THE MARTINS

David Foenkinos

Translated from French by Sam Taylor

David Foenkinos is the author of 17 novels. His books have been translated into 40 languages. His novel *Delicacy* was made into a film starring Audrey Tautou. He received the 2014 Prix Renaudot and Prix Goncourt des lycéens for *Charlotte*.

Sam Taylor is an author and former correspondent for *The Observer*. His translations include Laurent Binet's *HHhH*, Leïla Slimani's *Lullaby* and Maylis de Kerangal's *The Heart*, for which he won the French-American Foundation Translation Prize.

THE MARTINS

David Foenkinos

Translated from the French by Sam Taylor

Gallic Books
London

A Gallic Book

First published in France as *La famille Martin*
by Éditions Gallimard
Copyright © Éditions Gallimard, 2020
English translation copyright © Sam Taylor, 2022

First published in Great Britain in 2022 by Gallic Books,
12 Eccleston Street, London, SW1W 9LT

A CIP record for this book is available from the British Library
ISBN 978-19-13547-30-1

Typeset in Fournier MT by Gallic Books

Printed in the UK by CPI (CR0 4YY)
2 4 6 8 10 9 7 5 3 1

The value of coincidence equals the degree of its improbability.

Milan Kundera

I was struggling to write. I was going round in circles. For years I'd invented the stories I wrote, rarely tapping into reality. I was working on a novel about a writers' workshop. The action took place during a weekend devoted to words. But I couldn't find those words. My characters made my head spin with boredom. Any real-life story would be better than this, I thought. Any non-fictional existence. Often during book signings, readers would come up to me and say: 'You should write about my life – it's incredible!' This was almost certainly true. I could go into the street, stop the first person I met, ask them for a few biographical details, and whatever they told me would, I felt sure, inspire me more than anything I could make up myself. That was how it started. I actually told myself: go out into the street and the first person you see will be the subject of your next book.

There was a travel agency below my apartment; I walked past that strange, dimly lit office every day. One of the women who worked there would often come outside to smoke a cigarette. She would stand there, practically motionless, staring at her phone. I would sometimes wonder what she was thinking about, because I do believe that total strangers have lives of their own. So that day I went outside and thought: if she's there, on her cigarette break, she will be the heroine of my next novel.

But the smoker wasn't there. A minute sooner or later and I might have been her biographer. Instead my eye was caught by the sight of an elderly woman crossing the road, pulling a purple shopping trolley. This old woman didn't know it yet, but she had just entered the literary realm. She had just become the main character in my new book (assuming she agreed to my suggestion, of course). I could have waited for inspiration or for a more appealing character. But no, the rule I'd set myself was to write about *the first person I saw*. There was no alternative. I hoped that this orchestrated coincidence would lead to an exciting story, or towards the kind of insight that allows you to understand something important about life. I had great expectations for this woman.

I went up to her and apologised for bothering her. I spoke with the honeyed politeness of a salesman. She slowed down, looking surprised. I explained that I lived nearby, that I was a writer. When you stop someone who's walking, you have to get straight to the point. It's often said that old people are suspicious of strangers, but she immediately rewarded me with a big smile. I felt confident enough to tell her about my plan.

'So ... I'd like to write a book about you.'

'Sorry?'

'I know this might seem a bit strange, but ... It's a sort of challenge that I set myself. I live just over there,' I added, pointing to my apartment building. 'I'll spare you the details but basically I decided that I was going to write about the first person I met in the street.'

'I don't understand.'

'Could I buy you a coffee now so I can explain?'

'Now?'

'Yes.'

'I can't. I have to go home. I have things I need to put in the freezer.'

'Ah, right, I understand,' I replied, wondering if my story was already becoming pathetic. I was excited about the possibilities of my idea, yet here I was having to write about the necessity of not letting frozen products thaw. A few years after winning the Prix Renaudot, I felt the shiver of decline run down my spine.

I said I could wait for her in the café at the end of the street, but she told me to come with her instead. By asking me to follow her home, she immediately showed her trust in me. In her shoes, I would never have let a writer into my apartment that easily. Particularly a writer in search of inspiration.

A few minutes later I was sitting alone in her living room while she busied herself in the kitchen. To my surprise, I was overcome by emotion. Both my grandmothers had died years before; it had been a long time since I'd found myself in an old woman's apartment. Her home was so similar to my memories of theirs: the plastic tablecloth, the loudly ticking clock, the faces of grandchildren in gold-coloured frames. With a pang I remembered those visits. We never said much, but I enjoyed our conversations.

My heroine returned carrying a tray. On it was a cup and a few biscuits. She hadn't thought to have anything at all herself. To reassure her, I gave a brief summary of my career, but she didn't seem worried anyway. It had clearly not even crossed her mind that I might be an impostor or a manipulator, a dangerous man. Later I asked her why she'd been so trusting. 'You looked like a writer,' she replied, leaving me slightly confused. To me, most writers look lecherous or depressed. Sometimes both. Anyway, as far as this woman was concerned, I looked the way I was supposed to look.

I was impatient to discover the subject of my new novel. Who was she? First of all, I needed to know her family name.

'Tricot,' she said.

'Tricot, like knitting?'

'That's right.'

'And your first name?'

'Madeleine.'

So I was in the presence of Madeleine Tricot. I felt doubtful for a few seconds. It was not a name I could ever have invented. I have sometimes spent whole weeks trying to think up a character's name, convinced as I was that the sound of a name has an influence on a person's fate. It even helped me to understand certain temperaments. A Nathalie could never act like a Sabine. With every name I invented, I would weigh up the pros and cons. And now, suddenly, without any procrastination, I found myself with Madeleine Tricot. That's one advantage of reality: it saves time.

On the other hand, there is a fairly sizeable disadvantage: the lack of any alternative. I'd already written a novel about a grandmother and the issues of ageing. Was I going to be stuck with this theme again? It didn't really excite me, but I had to accept all the consequences of my plan. What would be the point if I started to sidestep reality? After thinking about it, I decided that it wasn't merely coincidence that I had met Madeleine: once writers hit on a favourite theme, they are doomed to keep writing about it for life.[1]

---

1. Then again, walking the streets of Paris's seventeenth arrondissement at ten in the morning, I was hardly likely to bump into a go-go dancer.

Madeleine had lived in the neighbourhood for forty-two years. It was possible I'd already seen her around, although her face didn't seem familiar. I was relatively new to the area, but I did spend hours walking the streets to help myself think. I was one of those novelists for whom writing is like annexing a territory.

Madeleine must know about the lives of lots of people around here, I thought. She must have seen children grow up and neighbours die; she must be aware of the ghosts of old bookshops hiding behind shiny new supermarkets. There is undoubtedly a certain pleasure to be found in spending your whole life in the same place. What struck me as a geographical prison was a world of familiar landmarks, protective and comforting. My excessive love of escape often led me to move house (I was also the kind of person who never took off their coat in a restaurant). The truth was that I preferred to leave behind the scenes of my past, whereas Madeleine was constantly surrounded by memories. When she walked past her daughters' school, she perhaps saw them running towards her again, throwing their arms around her neck and shouting 'Maman!'

While we weren't yet close, our discussion had got off to a good start. We conversed so effortlessly that, after a few minutes, it seemed to me that we had both forgotten the context of our meeting. This is confirmation of a simple fact: people like talking about themselves. A human being is a walking autobiographical novel. I sensed that Madeleine was thrilled by the idea someone might be interested in her. So where would we start? I didn't want to tell her which memories to unwrap first. In the end she asked: 'Should I tell you about my childhood?'

'If you like. But you don't have to. We could start with any period of your life.'

She looked slightly lost at this. She wanted me to guide her through the labyrinth of her past. But just as I was about to begin questioning her, she turned to look at a small framed photograph.

'We could talk about René, my husband,' she said. 'He died a long time ago … So he'd like it if we talked about him first.'

'Ah, okay …' I replied, noting that in addition to all my living readers, I now also had to please the dead.

Madeleine took a deep breath, like a diver, as if her memories were hiding somewhere at the bottom of the sea. And she started to talk. She'd met René in the late sixties, at a Bastille Day party held in a fire station. She and a friend of hers had gone to the party in search of some handsome hunk they could dance with. But it was a rather puny man who approached her. Madeleine immediately warmed to him. She sensed he was not the kind of man who was in the habit of chatting up strange girls. And she was right. He must have felt something rare, in his body or his heart, to have dared approach her like that.

René told her later the reasons for his attraction. According to him, she looked exactly like the actress Michèle Alfa. Just like me, Madeleine had never heard of Michèle Alfa. It was true that she didn't make many films after the war. When she found the actress's photograph in a magazine, young Madeleine was surprised: there was only a vague resemblance. At most, you could describe the two women as being slightly similar. But for René, Madeleine was practically Michèle Alfa's double. The source of his emotion went much further back, to a terrifying episode from his childhood. During the war, his mother had been part of a Resistance network. Pursued by the Milice, she had hidden her young son in a cinema.[2] Poor, frightened René

2. This story reminds me of the film director Claude Lelouch, who has often recounted how his own mother would leave him for entire days in darkened cinemas during the Occupation, leading him towards his future vocation.

had clung to the faces on the screen, and Michèle Alfa's became, for him, an unforgettably reassuring image. So it was that, over twenty years later, he glimpsed the ghost of his protector in the eyes of a woman at a firemen's ball. Madeleine asked him the title of the film. *L'aventure est au coin de la rue*, he replied: Adventure awaits at the corner of the street. I was stunned but tried not to show it. The title seemed to nod uncannily to the concept behind my new book.

Madeleine had been thirty-three at the time. All her female friends were already married with children. She thought perhaps it was time for her to 'settle down' too. She explained that she was using this expression – '*se ranger*' – with reference to the title of Simone de Beauvoir's book *Mémoires d'une jeune fille rangée*, which had been published in the years prior to her encounter with René. She didn't want to disrespect her husband's memory but preferred to be straightforward with me: at the time she had been motivated more by reason than by passion. It was nice and reassuring to be loved by a man who was so sure of his feelings for her; so nice that she was able to forget the truth of her own feelings. Over time, René's kindness and consideration won her heart and in the end there could be no doubt: Madeleine loved him. But she never felt for him the devastating rapture she had felt for her first love.

She paused for a moment, clearly reluctant to talk about something so painful. Some scars never heal, I thought. Of course I was intrigued by this allusion to an apparently tragic passion. In terms of my novel, it was a promising prospect. But she had shown so much spontaneous trust in me that I didn't want to rush her by asking her to elaborate on that brief mention. She would return to it later. And while I cannot now reveal the things that I learned in the weeks and months that followed, I can certainly say that this intense love affair would form an important part of my story.

For now, let's stick with René. After their first meeting at the party, they agreed to see each other again soon. A few months later, they were married. And a few years after that, they were parents. Stéphanie was born in 1974, Valérie in 1975. Back then, it was unusual to become a mother in one's late thirties. Madeleine had delayed the moment mostly for professional reasons. And while she enjoyed motherhood, she struggled with the consequences that it had on her career. She regarded this as an injustice perpetrated against women by a patriarchal society. 'And my husband started working longer hours, so I was often left alone with the children …' she said in a voice still tinged with bitterness. But it seemed fairly pointless to blame a dead man.

René probably didn't realise how frustrated his wife felt. He was proud of his career at the RATP, the Paris public transport company. After starting out as a train driver on the metro, he ended up as one of the RATP's highest-ranking executives. For him, the company was a second family, and retirement struck him like a guillotine blade. Madeleine found herself alone with a sad, lost man. 'He couldn't stand doing nothing,' she kept repeating, her voice growing quieter each time. He had died twenty years before, but when she spoke about him the emotion still seemed raw. René would get up each morning like a soldier without a war. His wife encouraged him to take evening classes or do volunteer work, but he rejected all her suggestions. In truth, he had been deeply wounded by the way all his former colleagues had gradually turned their backs on him. He came to realise that all these friendships he had developed over years were in fact hollow and meaningless, and everything seemed pointless, absurd. He was diagnosed with colon cancer, which enabled him to find a label for his vague sense of decline. His funeral took place barely a year after his retirement and many of his former colleagues turned up. Madeleine looked at them one by one, without a word. Some of them gave speeches at the ceremony, praising him as a moral, warm-hearted man, but René was no longer there to hear these belated proofs of undying friendship. His wife considered their behaviour pathetic but kept her thoughts to herself. Instead she basked in memories of the tenderness, the peaceful harmony that she and René had shared. They'd accomplished so much together, been through so many joyous and painful experiences, and now it was all over.

Madeleine talked about René in such a vivid way that I half expected him to join us in the living room at any moment. To me, this was the most beautiful form of posterity: continuing to exist in someone else's heart. I wondered how people coped with losing the love of their life. To spend forty or fifty years with someone, sometimes feeling as if they were your own reflection, and then one day the mirror is empty. You must reach out with your hand to touch the wind, feel strange movements in the bed, speak words that are transformed into a hollow conversation. You don't live alone, but with an absence.

After a while Madeleine said: 'Perhaps we could visit him at the cemetery?' I politely dodged this, claiming that I didn't feel I really belonged there. That was just an excuse. Above all, I didn't want to end up writing a novel whose main purpose was to water flowers by a graveside. I preferred to stick with the living. So I brought up the subject of her daughters. The mere mention of Stéphanie's name was enough to create a tension in the room. I couldn't question Madeleine directly; I had to be patient, certain that I would eventually succeed in clearing up any grey areas.

Stéphanie had gone to live in Boston after meeting an American man. Listening to Madeleine, you might have thought that her daughter was simply determined to marry a foreigner, as if any man would do as long as he wasn't French. Madeleine didn't seem to know very much about her son-in-law. The few times she'd seen him, he'd always been incredibly smiley. But according to her, his smile was like a crack in a wall: it was all you could see, blotting out all awareness of the wall itself or the house around it. He worked in a bank, but Stéphanie never went into any detail about him. All her conversations with her mother took place on Skype, and Madeleine despaired that she could only communicate with her daughter and her two granddaughters via a computer screen, that she couldn't hug or kiss them. And then there was the language problem: she couldn't understand why Stéphanie didn't speak French with her children. Madeleine would hear the little girls say 'Hello Mamie' or 'Happy birthday,

Mamie' in English. It was like another barrier that her daughter had built to keep her out.

Thankfully, Valérie lived locally and came to see her almost every day. Madeleine started to smile: 'There's one of them I never see, and the other one I see a bit too often!' Even if this wasn't laugh-out-loud funny, I considered it a good sign that my heroine had a sense of humour. But I also thought it admirable that a woman my own age should go to visit her mother so often, always asking her if she needed anything. Valérie must be dependable, I thought, the kind of person who shoulders all the responsibility for family difficulties, who lives a life of permanent self-sacrifice. This was pure speculation, however, since Madeleine didn't linger on the subject of her daughters. My overriding impression was of a distance between the two sisters. Later I would learn that they were no longer on speaking terms and discover the reasons for their conflict, which went back many years.

I was happy with our first conversation. My book was progressing more quickly than I could have hoped. All the same, I am always slightly suspicious of anything that comes easily; it seems to foretell disaster. I am a pessimist by nature; I prefer to anticipate disappointment. I was desperately hoping Madeleine's life would not end up as yet another unfinished novel.

For now, there was no reason to fear such an outcome. She opened up spontaneously and I let her drift through her memories, making no attempt to guide her. After quickly moving on from the subject of her daughters, she began to tell me about her professional life. She had worked as a dressmaker, notably for Karl Lagerfeld. I interrupted her: didn't she think it was strange that she'd ended up in that line of work when her surname, Tricot, meant 'knitting'? As if it was predestined ...[3] It quickly occurred to me that she must have had to put up with this kind of comment all her life, and that I was showing a sad lack of subtlety. But she explained that it was her husband's surname and that she'd already begun her career before she met him. It was true, however, that René had said to her on their second date: 'You're a dressmaker and my name is Tricot. We're made for

---

3. This is what is known as an aptronym: when a person's name seems appropriate to their occupation. You can find a whole list of celebrity aptronyms online, such as the sprinter Usain Bolt, the novelist Francine Prose and the sanitary engineer Thomas Crapper.

each other.' So he hadn't been very subtle or inventive either. But Madeleine had smiled, and sometimes a whole life can begin with a smile.

I took advantage of this turn in our conversation to ask her what she thought of Karl Lagerfeld. 'He was the simplest man imaginable,' she replied. 'No complexity at all. Completely transparent.' This was not really the image I had of him. Surreptitiously I allowed myself a little mental digression: this information was good news for my book. If ever Madeleine became a little dull – from a literary point of view, I mean – I could always sprinkle the book with juicy details about the famous German designer. Lagerfeld could be my GET OUT OF JAIL FREE card.

In a voice filled with wonder, she described what seemed to have been the best years of her life: the Chanel years. She would never forget Lagerfeld's arrival, at a moment when the fashion house had lost its prestige. There had even been talk of the company going bust. When the designer turned up for the first time, he silently walked through every floor of the building. To the Chanel employees, his wanderings seemed interminable. Nobody knew what he was going to do: would he agree to become the house's chief designer? He looked attentively at the fabrics, soaked up the atmosphere of the place. Madeleine thought him very handsome. In contrast to what you might expect, he was not a fast man. He was a book lover and he walked at the leisurely pace of someone turning the pages of a novel. At last he came over to Madeleine and asked her a few questions: How long had she worked there? What did she think of the company? How did she see the future? It was this that she had never forgotten about him: how straightforward and direct he was; the way he took the time to think, and to listen to those around him. That evening he'd returned with a few sketches. He hadn't said yes, but his agreement was implicit. And that was how Chanel was reborn.

Madeleine was in her late forties at the time. Her daughters were teenagers; they needed less looking after. So she was able to throw herself into her work as never before. She enjoyed the excitement of the fashion shows, when the whole team would be caught up in the hysteria backstage. Lagerfeld's muse in those years was the model Inès de La Fressange – a lovely, elegant woman, according to Madeleine. 'She even came to my leaving party! She didn't have to do that …' Once again, Madeleine appeared emotional when talking about the past. For her, it all seemed so close. There are certain periods in the distant past that you feel you can almost reach out and touch.

She smiled as she described some of the excesses of the fashion business. Each collection took on crazy proportions, driven by the feeling that they could invent an era with a scrap of fabric. This sent everyone slightly mad. She remembered so many arguments that, with the benefit of hindsight, seemed pointless, trivial; idiots fighting over passing fads … Well, they were all equal now, under the ground. Talk of this feverish past brought Madeleine to the contemplation of her humdrum present. Perhaps my project would bring a different dimension to her days. In any case she seemed pleased by my enthusiasm.

Then, gradually, she began pausing more often, growing vaguer in her recollections, repeating the same anecdotes. It was probably just tiredness: she had been talking for more than two hours. I didn't want to wear out my source. I suggested she have a rest but she pleaded with me to stay a little longer. Her daughter would be arriving soon.

9

Valérie was exactly how I'd imagined her. I hadn't seen any photographs but, listening to Madeleine, I'd conjured up an image in my head which turned out to be close to the reality. She was quite an elegant woman, although I could sense a weariness in her appearance. Then again, her attitude towards me probably influenced my first impression. She was immediately suspicious of me and made no attempt to disguise her feelings. This was understandable: her mother had brought a stranger home and that man was now pestering her with questions. Valérie probably took me for a conman, which is perhaps not that far from an accurate description of a writer.

She asked me again: 'So you met in the street, and my mother invited you to have tea in her apartment?'

'That's right.'

'Do you do that often, going into old ladies' homes?'

'Allow me to explain. I'm a writer ...'

Valérie went over to her mother.

'Are you all right, Maman?'

'I'm very well,' replied Madeleine with a smile of such intensity that it seemed to surprise her daughter.

In an attempt to defuse the tension, I typed my name into a search engine and handed my phone to Valérie. She was able to verify that I wasn't lying, that I'd already published a number of books, some of which had been quite successful. Taking advantage of this positive new impression, I explained again the reason for my presence. Open-mouthed, she said: 'A literary project? My mother ... a literary project?'

'Yes.'

'My mother? A literary project?'

'I know this is going to sound a little strange, but ... I decided to stop the first person I saw in the street ... and write about her.'

'And the first person you met was my mother?'

'Yes. I just thought that anybody's life could be fascinating ...'

'I suppose so. But who's going to be interested in my mother's stories? I mean, I'm her daughter and even I sometimes switch off when she's talking.'

'Believe me, it'll be good. She told me about your father, your sister ... Lagerfeld ...'

'Oh, so what did she say about my sister?'

'You see, even the way you asked me that ... the tension in your voice ... makes me think that—'

'Ah, I see. So your novel is going to dig up family secrets. All the painful stuff.'

'No, no ... I would never write anything you didn't want me to.'

'That's what they all say. I don't read many contemporary novels, but I can tell that writing is often a way of settling scores.'

'...'

I didn't know what to say. She wasn't wrong. Novels these days sell fewer and fewer copies, and naturally that encourages publishers to seek out controversies and juicy revelations. Was that a temptation for me too? I couldn't deny that I was hoping my heroine would share a few secrets to keep the reader turning the pages. Beneath my innocent-seeming enthusiasm for a grandmother's life, I was just a vampire with a thirst for tragedy. Let's be honest: nobody is interested in happiness.

'Nothing to say?' Valérie prompted me.

'Sorry, I was just thinking … I completely understand how you feel. You think what I'm interested in is pain and sadness. I'm going to be honest with you: I can't make any guarantees. Your mother has agreed to talk to me and I have to be free to report what she says. But she doesn't have to tell me everything …'

'You know perfectly well how this will go. You'll make her trust you. She's an old woman, there are things she doesn't understand …'

'Why are you saying that?' Madeleine interrupted coldly.

'Sorry, Maman. That's not what I meant. I just want to check what this gentleman's motivations are.'

'Again, I understand your reservations,' I told her. 'But my intentions are not bad …'

Valérie stared at me in silence before indicating that I should follow her into the kitchen. 'We'll be back in a minute,' she told her mother, who looked slightly shocked at being sidelined from a conversation about her. This must become a common occurrence as you get older: people talk about you as if your own opinion is irrelevant. As I followed Valérie, I thought about the vehement way she'd said 'There are things she doesn't understand.' What did she mean? It was as if she was afraid of something, afraid that her mother might inadvertently bring up subjects that were private or disturbing.

Once we reached the kitchen, she began speaking to me in a low voice. Visibly flustered, she issued a few standard words of warning before explaining that the book I planned to write about her mother would probably be complicated because she was losing her memory. Of course, I thought, everybody's memories become a little fuzzy as they get older. But Valérie added: 'She's in the early stages of Alzheimer's. It's still manageable, but I can see it getting worse day by day. She's forgetting names, parts of her life …' I hadn't noticed this at all. For two hours, Madeleine had navigated the waters of her past with perfect clarity. Valérie mentioned that it was possible her mother's mind had been stimulated by our first meeting, like those opening sessions with a psychiatrist that seem extraordinary: there's an ecstatic feeling of relief as you let everything out, and then gradually you realise, over time, that you are sinking deeper instead of rising from your rut.

Perhaps Madeleine had been happy to go diving into the depths of her memory, as if to prove to herself that she was a book whose every page she knew by heart.

'I think my project could only do her good,' I said to Valérie.

'I don't doubt it. And it's clear that it would be interesting for her to talk to you. But I'm afraid that after a while she'd be confronted with her inability to remember. Do you understand my anxiety? For now, my mother is fine. She doesn't know she's getting Alzheimer's. I just don't want your project to cause her pain ...'

Just then, she suddenly stopped talking, as if overwhelmed by emotion. She had struck me as suspicious, even slightly hostile, but I understood now that she was defending her mother; she was defending her the way an army defends a territory attacked by an enemy, losing a little more of their homeland every day. I smiled at her compassionately, but I felt ashamed of that smile because I knew it was deceptive. The truth was that I was thinking about my book. It's the same for any writer: the story is all that matters. My project had been to stop the first person I met and write about them, and the first person I'd met was someone who was losing her memory. The irony of this was not lost on me. But I immediately changed my mind; perhaps it would be fascinating to write about a person's memory as it crumbled and disappeared. I could leave blank pages, write contradictory chapters ...

I decided then that I would space out my visits, so as not to exhaust my heroine. I could simply spend time with her, without necessarily pumping her for information. We could take walks in the neighbourhood or go shopping at the supermarket; snatches of ordinary daily life; it might all be of interest. Valérie interrupted my mental ramblings.

'Of course I think it's wonderful that you want to write about my mother. I think it's a bit crazy, but still wonderful. I can see it would be like a gift for my children, but …'

'But what?'

'I wanted to suggest something.'

'Okay. Go ahead.'

'I imagine that, if you're writing about my mother, you'll want to question me too.'

'Yes, probably.'

'In that case, you could also write about me. Well, not just about me but my whole family. My husband, my children.'

'That's not really how I imagined my—'

'Your project is to follow a real person, right?'

'Yes.'

'But there's nothing stopping you from broadening the project to take in her family as well. I don't know if we'd be very interesting, but there would always be things to tell.'

'That's true, but—'

'Listen, I'm suggesting this to help you out. I don't want to have to tell you to go and find someone else in the street.'

'…'

She stopped speaking for a moment, then said: 'I can tell that your presence has been good for her. I saw it as soon as I arrived. But my intuition is telling me to make this suggestion. I don't want my mother to feel that your entire project depends on her. That scares me.'

'...'

I didn't know what to think about this. I saw Valérie's proposal as a sort of infidelity towards my first idea. But my project was to submit to chance, and there was no reason why I couldn't continue to follow the dictates of chance. Valérie spent a few minutes talking about the advantages of her proposal and I understood why she was doing this. She didn't want to get in the way of an adventure that, to judge from her mother's smile, was a source of real enthusiasm. But she wanted to take some of the pressure off a memory that was unstable, unreliable. Anyway, it seemed as if I didn't have much choice.

We went back into the living room and Valérie announced: 'It's all arranged, Maman. A writer is going to write about your life. That's exciting. And he's going to write about us too. In fact, I'm going to steal him from you tonight so he can have dinner with us at home ...' So that was it: I really had no choice. Then again, there was something relaxing about having characters prepared to take charge of the story.

10

And so I found myself having dinner with a family I didn't know. I generally avoided all uncomfortable social occasions, but here I was, in the most improbable situation I could imagine.

When she introduced me to her husband and children, Valérie told them that I was going to have dinner with them and write a book about them. They looked pretty astonished.

A girl, who'd been presented to me as Lola, muttered: 'What the hell is Maman up to now?'

To which her brother replied: 'I preferred it when she was doing pottery.'

Their mother cut them short with the words: 'I can hear you!'

Patrick, the husband, said nothing. He could have been welcoming, could have asked me what I would like to drink, seen the funny side of the situation, but he didn't. He looked like a man putting up with one of his wife's strange whims. He gave a doubtful little pout intended to show Valérie that he would agree to this absurd idea just to make her happy. But she was a persuasive person; within a few hours she had become the ambassador for my literary quest.

We sat at the table and there was a silence. Presumably they were all waiting for me to speak, to start asking questions. In the end I introduced myself in a few words before mumbling something about how I was mainly there so I could listen to them. But nobody wanted to speak.

Valérie, clearly embarrassed by her family's attitude, tried to undercut the tension: 'It's an intimidating situation, isn't it?'

I made a sort of reassuring hand gesture in an attempt to make them understand that I was not in a rush. I completely understood that it would take them a while to get used to the idea, and that perhaps I would have to win their trust before they felt comfortable telling me anything.

My attention turned to Patrick. He had the manner of a sensitive child who'd retreated inside a shell of toughness. He looked slightly older than Valérie, although they were actually born the same year. They had met at university. They'd instinctively been drawn to each other, but it certainly wasn't love at first sight. Without wishing to minimise their feelings, it seemed to me that this was what could be called a sensible kind of love. It had been Patrick's first major relationship. Before Valérie, he'd generally been rejected by girls. He'd had a difficult adolescence, apparently, although I would never find out more than that; whenever we talked after this, he would avoid discussing that complex period. All the same, I definitely sensed that the core of his personality – his lack of self-confidence – had been formed back then, between the ages of thirteen and sixteen, when he felt as if he was on the sidelines watching all his peers fall in and out of love. Sometimes all it takes is a few failures and you can become permanently immune to success.

Coerced by his wife's meaningful looks, Patrick was forced to start speaking. Instead of talking about his childhood or some other memory, he preferred to tell me about his day. He had worked for the past seventeen years at an insurance company. I tried to imagine what it must be like to live such a linear life, to go every day to the same place, see the same people, have the same conversations in front of the coffee machines (where you could also get soup). There must, I thought, be something reassuring about a career like that. In fact, Patrick's professional life was going through a difficult patch. A few months before, a new manager had taken over the company. Jean-Paul Desjoyaux was the caricature of a profit-obsessed mercenary. His goal was to check everything, all the time. To be more precise, he hunted down the smallest mistakes and used them as excuses to fire people without compensation. He also didn't hesitate to encourage his employees to denounce one another.

That morning, Desjoyaux had summoned Patrick to his office and told him that they would have a meeting in three days' time. This was torture. Why not just tell him there and then whatever he wanted to say? Patrick would spend the next few days with his stomach in knots. Desjoyaux's smooth, blank expression had given nothing away. It was psychological bullying honed to a fine art: a cold, almost cheerful method of professional termination. There had to be an element of sadism in his behaviour; given the general atmosphere at the company, he couldn't not be aware that telling an employee he would see him three days later meant that the employee was going to suffer in the meantime. Worse, he had added that it was *imperative* that they meet. Words have a meaning. Imperative meant this was major, decisive; it sounded like a death knell.

The evening we first met, Patrick was having dinner with his family while imagining that he would soon be unemployed. This was what had happened to Lambert, one of Patrick's colleagues: one day he'd had a job, the next day he had nothing. The company was downsizing. 'Don't worry,' everyone had told Lambert. 'You're young, you don't have any children, you'll bounce back easily.' But nothing was easy these days, least of all bouncing back. Patrick had bumped into Lambert two weeks earlier and had noticed that he was looking rather gaunt. Lambert had pretended everything was fine, but the look on his face said otherwise. Patrick, in turn, had pretended to believe what Lambert was telling him, so as not to embarrass him, but now he felt bad about this. He should have said: 'Listen, I can see that you're not okay. Let's go for a coffee and see what we can work out.' Instead he'd kept silent. He'd watched as Lambert disappeared into a metro entrance, swallowed up by the crowd.

Patrick had tried to call him but there was only an automated message stating that the number was no longer in service. Why would that have happened? Everybody kept their phone number. It was the motto of our age: always be reachable. Lambert must have been unable to pay his bills and so his line had been cancelled. There was no other explanation. So now Patrick had no way of contacting him; there was no possibility that they would ever have more than one of those superficial conversations between two ex-colleagues who bump into each other in the street and tell lies with forced smiles. These were Patrick's thoughts on the evening of our first encounter. In three days' time, it would perhaps be his turn. Perhaps he too would lose his phone number and nobody would be able to contact him any more. In three days' time, that ghoul Desjoyaux would explain why it was *imperative* that they meet.

Obviously, some of these details were given to me later by Patrick. But during that dinner, he did eventually get quite a lot off his chest. Valérie seemed surprised, particularly since the early part of the evening had given no clue as to what was coming. Clearly I had underestimated the need that every person felt to confide in a stranger, to express all that they had been bottling up prior to the moment an outsider offered a sympathetic ear. My role was not to make any comment or give advice, at least not yet. I simply nodded understandingly while maintaining the detachment necessary to transcribe all of this without being overly affected by it. It was probably this attitude that led Patrick to ask me: 'Are you really interested in all this stuff about Desjoyaux?'

'Yes, really. And I think my readers will be too. We all know a Desjoyaux,' I said earnestly.

I genuinely believed this. Not that we all have a psychopathic boss but, for me, all stories echo one another. I am often surprised by the degree to which readers find themselves in books, even those books with the strangest, most disturbing plots. We see reflections of our private reality everywhere we look. So, yes, I was certain that this Desjoyaux character would resonate as a symbol of the mistreatment that everyone has suffered at one time or another in their life. Surely, too, people would empathise with Patrick, this insecure man trying to stand firm in the face of deliberate humiliation. That was how I felt anyway.

Patrick finished speaking. He'd told me a great deal and I thanked him. After that, there was another silence. Who would narrate the next chapter of my book? During this pause in the conversation, I thought about Pirandello's play *Six Characters in Search of an Author*. I was drawn to this idea of inverting a creative situation, like a colour going off in search of a painter. Since my characters had an author sitting at their dining table, it was up to them to continue feeding me with words.

My enthusiasm was to be dampened by the couple's children. They showed absolutely no interest in me. We live in an age when everything seems normal. Is this because of television with its endless reality shows, enabling us to vicariously experience all sorts of improbable situations? Anything from police officers in a nudist camp to couples on the verge of divorce stranded on a desert island. If you can see or know everything there is to see and know, perhaps this inevitably leads to a lowering in the libido of curiosity; perhaps travel will one day lose its charm thanks to the existence of Google Maps. I thought about this as I observed the passive faces of the two teenagers. I tried to imagine how I would have felt if, at their age, my mother had invited a writer to have dinner with us; I think I would have wanted to know more about him, his motivations, and that I would even have tried to appear interesting (not an easy task given how little self-confidence I possessed at that age). I was surprised by their attitude, even knowing as I did that adolescence is an age when the outside world can sometimes seem as dull and pointless as a still life.

At fifteen, Jérémie looked as though he was carrying an immense weight on his shoulders. This impression was accentuated by the slowness of his movements. Even chewing food seemed like a herculean task. In other words, he was the living cliché of a sullen teenager. I started to wonder if fate had brought me into contact with the kind of hackneyed characters I could have invented for myself. A grandmother who was losing her memory, a slightly sad middle-aged woman, a man stressed out by his job, and now a miserable adolescent boy. Were these people the fruit of my weary imagination? No, they were real.

How could I pull my mind out of this downward spiral? I had to believe in the power of positive thinking. If you can persuade yourself that amazing things can happen, sometimes they actually will. I am fascinated by the kind of successful, happy people who say: 'I always believed in myself. I knew I would make it …' While self-confidence may not guarantee well-being, it is surely the most fertile soil for fulfilment. So I had to believe in my characters. I had to convince myself that beneath their apparent banality these people were hiding thrilling vices, were capable of unexpected acts that would render their existence captivating. Despite my initial premise – 'all lives are fascinating' – I was expecting something more from them. Then again, there must be a reader somewhere who would be enchanted by an analysis of the yawns of a Parisian teenager. A niche market, perhaps, but they do say there's an audience for everything.

Of course I could modify reality; it would be easy to add a few impromptu incidents, to invent some charming neuroses.

Is Romain Gary's memoir *Promise at Dawn* really an exact portrayal of his mother? Didn't the author exaggerate a bit when he described the tireless, overflowing affection that this woman felt for her son? The way she worshipped him as some sort of deity made her seem sublime and, let's be honest, fictional. In any autobiography there is a temptation to flirt with the realms of imagination.

Could Jérémie read my troubled mind? Just as I was thinking this, he sat up straight. It was quite strange seeing him like that: his posture changed completely, and there was a brighter look in his eyes.

'It is pretty cool,' he said. 'We've got our own official biographer.'

'Thank you,' I replied, unsure whether this was a compliment or just an observation.

'I'd have preferred Amélie Nothomb though.'

Not wanting to seem uptight, I smiled at this witticism. It was good news, after all: I had here a specimen of an endangered species, a teenager capable of making a literary reference. As it turned out, this burst of sociability would be Jérémie's only contribution to the evening. But I knew I shouldn't expect too much: one reply per meal was already pretty good going.

Not that he lacked encouragement. Valérie pushed her son to be a little more talkative. In the end he mumbled a joke about how he wished he had his own Wikipedia entry because that way he wouldn't have to introduce himself to people. (Unfortunately, it fell a little flat since it was hard to make out what he was saying.) Under sustained maternal pressure to open up, he finally sighed and said that his favourite colour was blue. I tried to match his wit by talking about how important this colour would be to my story, and my attempt at humour fell just as flat as Jérémie's had in the awkward silence that filled their dining room. Not that it mattered: I could wait for my new characters to come to me, as Madeleine and Patrick had. In truth, the same thing happens to me with fiction. I sometimes invent men or women who have no desire to do anything, and I have to submit to their will too. Or to what you might describe as my imagination being in a bad mood.

12

What would this dinner have been like if I hadn't been there? To have an idea, all I had to do was look at the large television that dominated the living room. I had infiltrated a tired family, trapped on the wheel of routine; passengers on the same ship who brushed past each other without ever really meeting. It was a common household tragedy, but no less painful for that. Was life really nothing more than this parade of weariness? I tried to imagine Valérie and Patrick falling in love, having sex, travelling together and envisaging a future when they would be the happy parents of two joyous little children. Where had all those dreams gone? I could write about this world submerged under the weight of years. I always see the past in the face of the present; I always see the child inside the adult, and the spark of passion in the dead-eyed stares of bored couples. Despite the somewhat reserved welcome they had given me, I was touched by these people; I sensed their fragility, and it echoed emotions that I too had felt. We were united in our stupefaction at the trials of ordinary life.

Valérie had invited me here to lighten the pressure on her mother, but perhaps also because she thought my presence would breathe new life into her family. Surely they were bound to be tickled by the absurdity of the situation? Nothing of the kind occurred, however, and I remained an intruder. I could sense that Valérie was trying to conceal her disappointment. Her son wasn't playing along. As for her daughter, Valérie knew in advance that she would make no effort. She had whispered to me as I entered the apartment: 'Lola's at a difficult age. She never wants to do anything with us any more.'

I can't say that Lola was unpleasant towards me, she was just completely indifferent. Her entire face radiated the desperate desire to be somewhere else. She was there without being there, to the point that I felt as if I were sitting opposite Malevich's painting of a white square on top of another white square.

She was seventeen and she didn't know what she wanted to do when she left school. According to her mother, this was a source of anxiety for Lola.

On that first evening, she refused to introduce herself, saying simply: 'I don't want you to write about me. That's my right.'

Of course, this immediately made me want to find out more. During dinner, I observed her on several occasions without managing to form an opinion. She might be sad, boring, intense, secretly enthralled, blasé, dreamy, melancholic, ambitious, creative … how could I know? Perhaps even she herself didn't know. Destiny, at her age, often looks like a rough sketch. She glanced at me a few times with eyes that seemed quite hard ('Who is this guy?') but I sensed a certain vulnerability ('Him and his stupid project are really getting on my nerves'). Deep down, I enjoyed wondering who she was and how she would develop in my book; it didn't bother me particularly if I had to wait until Chapter 45 or Chapter 114 to discover more about her. In fact she seemed very much like the kind of character who first appears in the middle of a novel, sparking a new storyline.

13

This dinner had not kept all its promises, but I could hardly expect every second spent with my characters to feed the literary beast. It was a project that had to bloom slowly, as things do in real life, with its silences and its moments that do not move the narrative along. Later, I could always decide to cut any really dull parts. Who would believe the account of a life that was always exciting, anyway? For most of our daily life, we weave adventures around the edges of boredom. I had to be satisfied with what they had shared with me so far, and to consider this a highly promising beginning. I was very keen on that idea of *promise*.

Given how dinner had gone, Valérie suggested that we meet for lunch the next day. She would be more free to talk to me. She wasn't wrong: I had underestimated that essential fact. There was probably little point in trying to interview all my protagonists at the same time. Encountered separately, they would be far more likely to open up; a bit like in those police interrogations where the suspects are questioned one by one so they can't compare stories or intimidate each other into silence.

And so, that evening, I left the Martin family. Yes, I forgot to mention: that is Patrick's surname. It's a very common family name in France; I'm not a mathematician so I can't calculate the odds that I would have ended up talking to someone called Martin, but they had to be pretty short. Usually the characters in my novels have more convoluted names. I particularly like names beginning with K; I always have the impression that a K will help my heroes to be more exciting. So I can't deny that I found it somewhat worrying to have ended up with a family of Martins. Could I really write a good novel about people called Martin?

To reassure myself, as I took the metro home I typed their full names into a search engine on my phone. I was instantly buried under an avalanche of Patrick Martins and Valérie Martins. I was very happy about this. First of all, it's an ideal surname if you never want to be found on Facebook. If a psychopath happened to meet a Valérie Martin one evening, he'd have a struggle on his hands to track her down afterwards. People named Martin have the power of anonymity, which obviously gives them the ability to exist as part of a multitude. They are the Chinese of names. And there is something undeniably novelistic about that.

I wanted to check out a few of my characters' namesakes. Partly to find out which among them had managed to stand out from the crowd. (What can I say? I'm a curious person.) Among the hundreds of Patrick Martins, the most visible was a big business leader. Not only that but he was vice-president of Medef, the French federation of employers. It was true, I thought: Martin did sound like a leader's name. The kind of person who could talk fluently about employee savings schemes and planned redundancies. For Valérie Martin, my eye was caught by an osteopath in Verrières-le-Buisson. If you had a slipped disc, what could be more reassuring than a Valérie Martin? Nobody with that name would ever mess up your back. It was also true that Verrières-le-Buisson contributed to this comforting image. Windows-in-the-bush. It was such a cosy name (at least in French). So easy to imagine myself drinking jasmine tea in Valérie Martin's waiting room ... I noted down the address for my next lumbago and then continued my research. For Jérémie Martin, too, there were many applicants to choose from. In the end I selected a regional councillor in south-east France, the council chairwoman's right-hand man. Clearly, the Martins were a powerful family. Dependable too. 'Call Jérémie Martin,' I imagined the chairwoman saying. 'We have a problem with council houses in Marseille.' 'But he's on holiday …' 'I said call him!' How right she was. Jérémie Martin was exactly the kind of guy who would interrupt his holiday to deal with a crisis at work. He would leave the Balearic Islands right away, with his files under his arm. His wife and three children would accompany him to the airport and wave goodbye to him, their arms moving in astonishingly perfect synchronisation. When he got back to the office, he would tell the chairwoman: 'Don't worry, I've got this.' And everyone would feel so much better.

When I typed in Lola Martin's name, I got a little surprise: a beguine singer.[4] I could hardly hope for better than a beguine singer! I immediately listened to her song 'Ti Paule', an ode to Martinique so evocative that I could practically smell the rum punch and the easy living. As I streamed a few of Lola Martin's songs, I also read some of the comments about her. Pimpky 46 posted: 'Pure sunlight in my ears! And it can't be easy for a girl to succeed like this in such a man's world. Respect and Love!' How courageous this Lola was. And always smiling: the elegance of a fighter incarnate.

I looked through pages and pages of Martins to reassure myself. I don't know why I have such an anxious relationship with names. It was the same with Madeleine Tricot. I almost have the impression that the most important thing for any character is their name. Everything else flows from that. The fact that I hadn't chosen these characters' names made me feel like the father of a child who'd already been named. So I'd wanted to observe a few

4. Admittedly her next-door neighbour in this web search was in charge of customer relations at the BRED cooperative bank.

different Martin lives, particularly those with the same first names as my characters, to assess their literary potential. Reassured by my search results, I ended up feeling very happy with my little Martin family.

14

I got home just before eleven. My laptop was open on my desk. I was able to read the last words I'd written before giving up. A few hours prior to this, I'd felt almost physically sick of fiction and had gone outside to find a story in the street. All of this seemed crazy or at least rather odd, but what did it matter? There's no point trying to label our intuitions. All I knew was that I now had an entire family at my disposal. Five characters whose life stories I could tell. I was already excited at the idea of seeing them again and finding out more about them. For the moment, I typed up a brief summary.

WHAT I KNOW ABOUT MY CHARACTERS (1)

Madeleine Tricot, about 80 years old (I didn't ask her exact age). Widow. Two daughters: Valérie and Stéphanie, who lives abroad. There seems to have been a falling-out between the two sisters. Madeleine worked in fashion and has a few stories about Karl Lagerfeld (need to find out more). Mentioned a tragic first love. Can't wait to hear about that. Has memory problems. Early stages of Alzheimer's according to her daughter. But I didn't notice anything amiss.

Valérie Martin, 45. Married, two children. To take the pressure off her mother, she decided I should also write about her and her family. Occupation: history and geography teacher at a secondary school in the deprived outskirts of Paris. Often goes to see her mother. Doesn't seem very happy.

Patrick Martin. Same age as his wife. Works in insurance. Was summoned to a meeting in three days' time by his boss Desjoyaux (check spelling). Fears he'll be fired. Seems the pessimistic, anxious type. Distinguishing features: has a moustache (I don't know yet whether this will prove significant but I'm noting it just in case).

Jérémie Martin, 15. Typical teenager: lazy and lethargic. Does seem to have a sense of humour though.

Lola Martin, 17. Secretive. Barely spoke during dinner. Beyond her suspicion towards me, she struck me as being miles away, lost in her own thoughts. I don't want to get ahead of myself but she seems like the kind of person who has a secret.

I had strange dreams that night. The entire Martin family was angry with me; they were even threatening to kill me. This was the first time I'd ever been persecuted by my characters. Yet I felt as if I'd acted respectfully, that I hadn't done anything without their consent. Why did my subconscious feel so tormented? Writing is a form of betrayal. Becoming a writer is the fate of the guilty. Perhaps I was anticipating a moment yet to occur, when my characters would rebel against what I'd written about them. I woke with the sour taste of a premonition in my mouth.

Valérie had suggested I meet her at work so we could have lunch together. She seemed to have taken my project to heart, and this made me even more sure that I had been right to accept her proposal. All the same, I wasn't about to abandon my initial source; I was planning to visit Madeleine that afternoon. My life now consisted of nothing but meetings with members of the same family.

As I left my apartment, I saw the travel agency woman outside, smoking a cigarette. The woman I had thought, the day before, might have been my heroine. What if I wrote a second book, in parallel, about her? I could follow several stories and then pick the most interesting ... No, impossible. I had to stay faithful to my original idea, and more than that, to chance. I immediately abandoned these thoughts of literary infidelity.

Anyway, in a bookish sense, I liked Valérie. I'd always been attracted to characters who were neither one thing nor the other. Not happy, not unhappy, but stagnating in a strange zone in between, where the question of personal fulfilment becomes lost in the maze of the passing years. And yet you sense that this cannot go on. The accumulated frustrations are starting to become unbearable. You sense that it all could blow up at any moment. The smile with which she greeted me only accentuated this feeling. I saw her waving to me even though she was quite a long way off, at the back of the school playground. She walked quickly towards me, as if relieved to have an opportunity to flee her workplace for an hour.

She usually ate at the school cafeteria, in a room for teachers only. They would talk about the students and their problems, which meant she never really got a break from work. Valérie could have eaten lunch alone in a nearby restaurant, to give herself some breathing space. But if anyone had seen her, it might not have looked good. They might have seen her solo dining arrangement as a form of disobedience to the diktat of collective responsibility. The need for solitude is often considered antisocial. Human relations are complicated, and sometimes we go against our own desires to avoid having to justify the choices we have made. So Valérie never took time out for herself at lunch, instead submitting to the unspoken obligation to spend it with her colleagues. This explained her enthusiasm. The fact that she had a meeting 'outside' was a legitimate excuse to leave her post, a perfect alibi.

17

We sat in a soulless café where music videos played on a large television screen at the back of the room. It seemed to me that Valérie had made an effort with her appearance, though the changes weren't obvious enough for me to be sure. Perhaps she wanted to be at her best for my book.[5] I had planned to make the most of our time together by asking her lots of questions, but she beat me to it.

'I bought one of your books this morning.'

'Oh, thank you. I could have given you a copy.'

'Don't thank me. I just wanted to find out a bit more about the man I'm going to be telling my life story.'

'Perfectly understandable. But I don't talk about myself much in my novels.'

'Yes, I could tell it wasn't very autobiographical. All the same, I thought it would allow me to get a handle on you. Through the tone, for example. I've only read a few pages but I get the impression that there's a sort of world-weary irony.'

'Ah, yes … maybe. That's what you sensed.'

'Are you slightly depressed?' she asked with a smile.

'Me? No … not at all.'

'You have a depressed man's sense of humour.'

'If you say so.'

'I actually like that. It's charming.'

---

5. She didn't know that I never give much in the way of physical descriptions of my characters.

'Thank you.'

'Can I ask you a personal question?'

'Yes.'

'Are you married?'

'…'

I could easily have omitted this exchange from my book, along with my response to it. I could have stuck purely to conversations about the Martin family. But I don't want to hide any interactions; they are part of my project. By involving myself in the lives of others, I become a protagonist. So I couldn't rule out the possibility that I would end up being a character in my own story.

But now I had to reply. What should I say? I have always found it difficult talking about myself. Not only are my novels not very autobiographical, but neither are my human relationships. I have never felt the need to open up to anybody. Of course, advice or comfort from a loved one can be a source of solace in difficult moments. But I have the sense that there is nothing to say when you are suffering. I have often healed in silence. And there's something else too … Perhaps this will sound strange, but I feel as if I know myself better than anybody else could; I see my own mistakes and faults; I am under no illusions about the aspects of my personality that are lacking. So I keep my private life private. Sometimes I will tell people things – over lunch with friends, for example – but only because I know I have to play my part in the obligatory sharing of confessions. There's probably nothing very surprising about the fact that writing has become my obsession; it remains the best way of travelling beyond the confines of my own personality. I am much more interested in escaping myself than understanding myself. But now I had to describe my love life to Valérie – and, by extension, to the reader. That's always the way it is: you can't avoid these questions. You must constantly tell people who you are, what you love, what you do, and whether you're alone or part of a couple. Even though, for me, the idea of revealing myself is a bit like going on holiday in the street where I live.

I was paralysed by Valérie's question. I thought about what she'd said – that my sense of humour was 'charming'. That didn't seem like a good sign. Already this lunch had taken a turn for the worse. I was here to write about her, not cause any trouble. This was the problem with real people: you had to keep them at an appropriate distance. If you were too cold, nothing would happen, but if you were too warm you risked the integrity of the story. I didn't have this problem with my other books; my fictional characters never tried to start up a relationship with me. Can you imagine Juliet asking Shakespeare if he was married? I began to doubt my ability to go through with this project. Not to mention the fact that Valérie must really be quite unhappy if she found me charming. My seductiveness had, for some time, resembled a Bergman film (without the subtitles).

I had to stop procrastinating and just act as naturally as I could. 'I'm not married,' I replied. 'I recently became single again.' I could see from the look on Valérie's face that she wanted to know more. In any case, she was waiting for me to elaborate on this bald statement. Which I did. My last girlfriend had decided to leave me after six years together. The end had come suddenly. True, we'd had our ups and downs, but for a long time I'd thought what we had was genuine and passionate, and that the wanderings of our hearts did not alter one essential truth: we loved each other. I told Valérie all this because I had no choice; if I wanted to receive, I first had to give. After a while, she interrupted me.

'I'm sorry to ask you this, but are you sure she didn't meet someone else?'

'I don't think so.'

'You don't think so?'

'No. In fact, I'm sure she didn't. She would have told me.'

'People often lie when they're splitting up.'

'Well, not in our case.'

I then said '*voilà*', indicating that I wished to move on from this subject. I didn't want to keep talking about it. I didn't want to tell her that Marie had left me with the words: 'I prefer solitude to you.' Yes, that was what she said. Her words had made me very angry. But I imagine she'd said them to hurt me, since I hadn't reacted to all the signals she'd been sending me: that she was sad, that she was falling out of love with me, that she wasn't happy or fulfilled. The truth was, I hadn't understood those signals. It was only when she left me that I realised what they'd meant. Sitting in the café with Valérie, I felt engulfed by a wave of melancholy – an emotion that I thought I had finally purged from my life several weeks before.

Thankfully, Valérie, with perfect tact, cut short my musings with the words: 'You must be unbearable. I mean, it has to be awful, living with a writer …'

'…'

'But at least something must always be happening with you.'

At last she was pulling the blanket of the conversation over to her side. An allusion to her dismal marriage. But she said this with a smile. Irony is often the gateway to despair. For her, the description of my break-up had been evidence of an exciting life. When you aren't happy, other people's lives always seem much more interesting; your judgement on such matters is impaired, to say the least. If I'd told her that I had cancer, she would probably have said: 'Oh, that's great! At least something's happening in your body!' More than ever, I had the feeling that I had entered this woman's life at a critical moment.

18

Now that we'd discussed my love life to Valérie's satisfaction, it was time to focus on her. But I had to be methodical. I couldn't just let her give me some vague biographical background and a mishmash of recent emotions. She understood and obediently complied. First of all, I wanted to understand the context of her professional life. She had been working at the Collège Karl-Marx in Villejuif for twelve years now, taking the metro every morning. I had the sense that this relentless routine had gradually worn away her passion for the job, year after year. Her eyes shone when she talked about studying History at university and her early years as a teacher. She wasn't sure when things had started to go wrong, but she did remember one September the immense weariness she'd felt at the idea of returning to work. That summer had seemed especially brief.

Perhaps her job was simply harder than it had been before? I'd been hearing more and more stories of parents complaining about their children's schools, sometimes even becoming violent. Teachers were, increasingly, lightning rods for a society in crisis. But Valérie said it was nothing like that. She'd never had any serious problems at work and most of her pupils were attentive and eager to learn. She'd been offered a job in Paris, closer to where she lived, but she'd preferred to stay at the school in Villejuif where everything was familiar and she was happy to follow the progress of her favourite students. So why had she lost her love of teaching?

A few months before this, she'd confided in a colleague, a slightly older woman who taught Spanish at the school and with whom she'd become friends. 'What you're feeling is completely normal,' the woman had told her. 'All teachers go through this at some point. It's a job with a fixed calendar: back to school in September, holidays on the same dates ... It's easy to feel like the years are blurring into one, that life has lost its flavour. But you're the one who has to change that. You could take your students on a school outing, do something different, be innovative ...' Her colleague had been right: Valérie had let the routine suffocate her without even trying to fight it. Yet the truth was that she had quite a lot of freedom. In the end, she'd decided to take her pupils to Auschwitz. That had brought the class together. The children had been transformed by their shared journey into the memory of horror. And yet she vividly remembered feeling haunted by a sense of absolute emptiness as she sat in her hotel room in Krakow that evening. Something was missing in her life, but what it was she didn't know.

As if embarrassed by these confessions, Valérie suddenly changed the subject. She wanted to talk about me again.

'Obviously I don't know you. But I mentioned you to my colleague who teaches French and she would be thrilled if you'd agree to meet her students.'

'Yes, maybe later. For now, I need to devote myself to this book. And that means talking about you.'

'Are you really interested?'

'Your husband asked me the same question.'

'Well, that's something we have in common,' she said with unveiled sarcasm.

'And yes, of course I'm really interested. Weariness is an important subject these days. Probably because our relationship with fulfilment has completely changed.'

'What do you mean?'

'Nowadays it's everyone's ambition to be happy. That's obviously changed our expectations.'

'If you say so.'

'Lots of people I know are changing their occupations. Retraining has become the norm. People reach forty and realise they don't want to work as an estate agent any more – they'd rather teach yoga. I see it all the time. Why should teachers be any different? Just because they're employed by the State? What you're feeling seems perfectly understandable to me. Maybe you want a change of career.'

'Well, not yoga, that's for sure! What bothers me is not feeling that passion for my job any more. I don't think I really want to change, I just want to feel that spark again.'

'I know exactly what you mean.'

'Anyway, you're right about people having fragmented careers. I have a friend who was a paediatrician and she gave it all up to open a cheese shop in Corsica! She's an amazing woman. You should write about her instead of me. If you're ever disappointed with me, I'll give you her number.'

'You're not disappointing,' I said without thinking.

Valérie seemed pleased by this unusual compliment. Perhaps it made her feel like an interesting heroine. I hadn't intended to put so much of myself into our conversation; I wanted to remain withdrawn, to be a listener. But the discussion had hit a nerve for me. I knew that feeling all too well – losing one's spark. Many times, writing a novel, I have felt lost, completely lacking in motivation. And then one day, like a miracle, my love of words would return. A writer can quickly become bipolar. So I understood Valérie and what she was describing: that feeling of paralysis, doing a job drained of all colour.

19

The conversation continued; soon it would be time to leave. I could have waited until our next meeting to ask her about her sister, but I couldn't stop thinking about it.

'Could I ask you about something else?'

'Yes, of course.'

'I sensed yesterday that there was an awkwardness when I mentioned Stéphanie. Your mother seemed uncomfortable too.'

'...'

'What happened?'

'There are some things I don't feel like talking about.'

'I understand.'

'Don't sulk. I promised I'd be honest, and I will be. But it's too early to talk about my sister.'

I felt annoyed with myself. I'd known this was a sensitive, even painful subject, and yet I'd clumsily blundered into it at the end of the meal. I should have been more tactful. She had already opened up so much, and she'd let me into her family. I made it clear that she would be the one to decide when and how much she wanted to tell me. I felt certain that the best way to get people to talk was not to pressure them too much. I had the same attitude towards writing, in fact: if I couldn't find the right words, I wouldn't keep racking my brains – I'd just wait for the words to come to me.

We left the restaurant like two friends who have lunch together occasionally. The conversation had flowed easily, and I'd have been happy if she'd wanted to keep talking. But Valérie was already late for her next class. I held out my hand, but she kissed me on the cheek and said: 'See you at home tonight!' She walked away quickly, looking cheerful, but after a few steps she turned around. 'There's something I have to tell you … I don't think I love my husband any more. I'm going to leave him. It's important you know that … for your book.' Then she walked away again as if what she'd said had been nothing of consequence; just a semicolon in a novel.

I was stunned. Why had she announced that so suddenly? Without even giving me the chance to respond. Then I thought maybe she'd acted that way to make my story more intriguing. She'd actually said: 'It's important you know that for your book.' So she'd told me a secret to help me with my project. I had sensed several times during lunch that she feared her life wasn't wild enough, and I'd had to reassure her on that point. Had she made that declaration to prove she wasn't boring? Did she really believe what she'd said? The couple I'd had dinner with had seemed tired, unenthusiastic about their daily life. But all the same it struck me as odd that she would reveal something so intimate. Despite the pact we'd made, I was still a stranger. I started to think that it was perhaps my presence that was pushing her to put words to what she was feeling. By getting her to talk about herself, I had driven her to a new lucidity. I hadn't foreseen that aspect of the situation, but now I could see it clearly: my intrusion into the Martin family was going to wreak havoc.

Valérie would tell me certain details a little later. Her husband no longer touched her. Her sensual life was dead. Yes, that was what she said: *my sensual life is dead*. There was so much violence in those words. You can die from not being looked at.

Yet Valérie felt sure she was still attractive. Pierre, one of her colleagues, had been flirting with her more and more openly. He would compliment her on the way she looked or suggest they go for a drink after work. She was not insensible to male attention, but deep down she couldn't help finding the whole thing slightly pathetic. She didn't want to have sex in a Villejuif hotel after classes with a man who didn't really turn her on and who had no intention of leaving his wife for her. She found adultery repellent. She wanted to be touched, but not at any price. Her life might be loveless, but it wasn't worthless.

She sent Pierre packing, and he ended up sleeping with Malika, the careers advisor. Valérie was disgusted that everyone knew about their fling; she would have hated being the subject of such seedy gossip. She imagined those two sad bodies joined in various positions for a few weeks, a few months at most. There was no chance that Pierre and Malika would suddenly be overcome by an all-consuming passion. No, nothing like that could happen. Their story had already been written and its ending was entirely predictable. However, there had been one surprising development: Pierre's wife had found out about her husband's affair. That, at least, might have led to a marital drama ... but no, even that was apparently too much to expect. To Valérie, this seemed the ultimate proof of weariness: not even to react when your spouse rejects your body in favour of another. With all the folly of human complexity, Pierre had been wounded by this. He'd wanted his wife to react, at least to say something, but she never did.

Valérie felt sure that her husband wouldn't have been like that. He might not touch her any more, but he would have been devastated by the idea that his wife could cheat on him. It made her feel good to think that. Well, that was what she imagined anyway; sometimes she worried that the opposite was true, that he wouldn't really care. But she preferred to think that he would be jealous. It was perhaps all that remained to them, the feeling that they still belonged to each other a little bit.

22

After lunch, I decided to go and see Madeleine. She opened the door to me with a wide smile, then immediately disappeared into the kitchen to make some tea. It was like a replay of the previous day's scene. Once again, sitting in the living room, I thought about my grandmothers. I had wondered so many times how they filled their days. It was the same with Madeleine. What did she do to get through all the empty hours? She went shopping, went for walks, saw her daughter and sometimes her grandchildren, and I imagined that she also watched television (one of my grandmothers would spend her entire day in front of TF1). Could you fill up a life that way? How did your relationship with time change once your days were numbered? I am obsessed by these questions.

When she reappeared, I asked her if she'd had a good morning. She replied instantly: 'Oh, I haven't stopped!' I still didn't know what exactly she had been doing with her time, but at least I had my answer. She didn't feel bored. In fact, it is surprising how seldom elderly people experience boredom. Unlike children, who complain about every minute not packed with activity. You probably have a different relationship with time once you reach a certain age, a relationship no longer characterised by submission to an occupation. I remembered how one day I had looked through my grandmother's window (she lived on the ground floor) and seen her sitting on the sofa doing nothing. She almost looked like she was meditating, but in fact she was just taking a brief holiday from herself. And I could read all sorts of emotions on her face, but boredom wasn't one of them.

Just as I was about to begin questioning her, Madeleine asked: 'How did it go at my daughter's house last night?'

'Very well.'

'What did you think of her husband?'

'Very nice,' I felt obliged to reply, out of a desire to remain neutral.

'And Jérémie? I bet he never stopped talking!'

'…'

Were we discussing the same person? Of course, people behave differently in different company, but all the same I found it hard to imagine that silent teenager as a friendly chatterbox. Maybe he saved all the words that bubbled up inside him so he could inundate his grandmother with them? Madeleine told me she was happy that I was going to write about the rest of her family. It was a relief not to feel that I was expecting too much of her. This was exactly what Valérie had said. And in fact I soon realised that Valérie had been right about her mother's faltering memory. During that second meeting, I noticed a few little absences. It wasn't much, and perhaps I was focusing on it after what her daughter had told me, but I did get the impression that Madeleine was struggling at times to find her words.

I suggested that we could look through some photograph albums together. And so we set sail on a voyage into the past. There were so many pictures of her daughters. I saw Valérie aged seven or eight. It was strange to think I'd just eaten lunch with the adult version of that child. Examining the photograph, I saw what seemed like a gleam of sadness in her eyes, a look that echoed the sadness I'd perceived in her during our lunch date. Was it possible to detect hints of a child's future in their expression? No, my gaze must have been contaminated by today's Valérie. In one of the pictures, her sister was holding her hand. Stéphanie appeared sunnier than Valérie, but the kind of sun that dazzles and blinds.

There were so many other memories to look through. I came across one of Madeleine's wedding photographs, in black and white of course.[6] That made me want to ask about René again. But I didn't want to hurt my host. I imagine the pain of remembering what no longer exists. Widows and widowers pretend to get used to the horror of living without their partner, out of a sort of human politeness, but the truth is that their hearts have been torn out. In fact, as soon as Madeleine began speaking of her husband, I got the same impression I'd had the day before. She had loved spending her life with him, but it had been a marriage devoid of passion. She spoke of him as if he were a travelling companion, almost a friend. She talked about how self-effacing he was, even at the end: 'He suffered, but he passed away so calmly, in his sleep.' Then she added with a sigh: 'The dream …'

So that was it, the ultimate dream of a person's life: dying in one's sleep.

Once she'd pointed out this aspect of her husband's character, I could discern it in the photographs. René was always in the background, a strange and not entirely convincing little smile on his face, as if he were embarrassed to be there; more a shadow than a man. Once again, she told me about René's passion for his work. He had adored the RATP. He knew every story about the metro stations; nothing excited him more than line extensions. The day they announced that Line 7 would go all the way to Villejuif … that had been his moon landing. According to Madeleine, the source of this rectilinear obsession could be traced directly back to his childhood. She repeated the anecdote about him having

---

6. It's incredible how well black and white suits certain situations; it emphasises the colourlessness of some occasions.

to hide in a cinema, stressing that this had happened on many occasions. He had grown up with the terror of always having to hide, never sleeping in the same place, his guts twisted in fear. In the end, his mother had been arrested after being denounced by a member of her own network. She had died soon afterwards, probably while being tortured; but that was only a theory. His family had never been able to find out the truth. Madeleine felt certain that it was during this disjointed, unsettled childhood that René's love of the straight line had been born. An odd theory, but not implausible. The metro is, after all, the path from which one can never stray. It is the reassuring journey par excellence; an antidote to all wanderings and hunts.

Unsurprisingly, René hated change. Their life together was marked by regular rhythms and familiar settings. Every summer, they would go on holiday to the same place: a campsite in Vichy. 'For its thermal spas,' she made clear, having guessed from the look on my face that I associated that city with wartime collaboration. I did think it strange that a man who had lost his mother during the war would want to spend all his holidays there. The more she told me about her husband, and his taste for the predictable, the more disconcerting I found it. There is something fantastical about ordinary life. Furthermore, most psychopaths lead existences as orderly as a Bach concerto. I didn't share this insight with Madeleine, of course, but she seemed happy that I found her husband interesting. It was as if I were offering him some sort of posthumous glory.

Although Madeleine sometimes appeared to be roaming through a parallel world, lost in some unimaginable sensation from her past, she looked me straight in the eyes when she told me: 'René was a good husband and a good father, but the man I loved most was called Yves. I met him when I was twenty-two, and for three years we had a wonderful relationship. But then he suddenly left me. He went to live in the United States. I was in agony. That was the most painful period of my life …' Abruptly she stopped speaking. Some stories have to end that way, as if guillotined by emotion. I didn't know what to say. Naturally I wanted to question her more about this man, to understand what lay behind their separation, but above all I felt moved. She had spoken about him with such intensity. And I was touched by her trust in me. I was a stranger, yet she was revealing to me the most heart-rending part of her life.

After a long silence, I finally asked her: 'Didn't you ever try to find out what had happened to him?'

'No. And I never saw him again. Although … there was one time when I almost saw him.'

'When was that?'

'I don't remember exactly. The girls must have been ten or twelve. I received a note at my atelier. I was working for Chanel. I'm not sure how he managed to find me there. I'd changed my surname …'

'He knew that you worked in fashion. Maybe he called up all the fashion houses, asking for Madeleine.'

'But we were all called Madeleine back then!'

'Well, anyway, he looked for you and he found you. So what happened?'

'Nothing.'

'Tell me more.'

'He wrote me a note because he was in Paris, saying he'd be happy to see me again. That was all, just a few lines, with the name of his hotel. After so many years of silence. I suppose I might have been thrilled, but I wasn't. In fact, I was angry with him for suddenly reappearing like that. I had my own life by then: my job, my daughters. I'd got back on my feet. It wasn't nice of him to do that. I decided I wouldn't go. And I held firm, but ...'

'You went anyway?'

'Yes. The desire was too strong. Besides, I needed to know why he'd left me the way he did. Not understanding had driven me crazy. So I went to his hotel ...'

'And?'

'Nothing. He'd left that morning. And that was that. Fate hadn't wanted us to meet again. It left me feeling helpless and confused again. I was obsessed by the idea of this meeting that almost happened.'

'That's terrible. He hadn't left you a note, an address where you could reach him?'

'No. Since I hadn't gone to see him, I imagine he thought it better not to leave any trace behind.'

'And that was all?'

'Yes.'

'You never tried to find him again?'

'How?'

'I don't know. You could have looked for him on the internet. Facebook, for example ... What's his surname?'

'Grimbert.'

'Would you like me to try?'

'Try what?'

'To find him.'

'...'

Madeleine made a movement with her head that I took for a nod of assent. I opened Facebook on my phone. I found a few Yves Grimberts, but only one appeared to be the same age as Madeleine. The investigation could hardly have been any faster. Modern technology must have put so many private detectives out of a job. The age of stake-outs is over. The man's profile said that he lived in Los Angeles. I asked Madeleine if she wanted to see his photograph, and she nodded again. Without any sign of emotion, she said: 'That's him.' She must have been in shock. She continued to stare at her first love before finally adding: 'He hasn't changed.' I would never have dared use that line in a novel. I thought it was beautiful that she could say that about this man, almost sixty years after the last time she'd seen him. The power of a feeling is capable of stopping time.

I thought she would want to know more about him. It wouldn't have been difficult to dig a little deeper. But what she'd just seen appeared to have stolen all her energy. She said she wanted to rest now, and I understood perfectly. As she walked me to the door, she said: 'Thank you.' I hadn't done anything special – just typed a name into my phone. At the last moment, she held me back. 'I know I'm old and tired,' she said, 'and that sometimes I get a bit mixed up, but there's one thing I'm sure of: I want to see Yves again. I want to see him again before I die.'

24

After leaving the apartment, I went downstairs, walking more and more slowly until finally I sat down on a step. I had been staggered by Madeleine's last words: 'Before I die.' As soon as she saw that man's photograph, she immediately decided she had one final act to accomplish. My questions had, unwittingly, triggered an unstoppable desire. And of course – why deny it? – I thought about my book. Perhaps this, and this alone, was my story? I already saw myself flying to the United States with Madeleine to describe the joy of their reunion.

This story reminded me of a newspaper article I'd read recently, with photographs that had been published all over the world, touching the hearts of everyone who saw them. Seventy-five years after the Normandy Landings, an American man had rediscovered the woman he'd loved. Stunned by this miracle of fate, the two of them had held hands, their eyes full of tears. The passing of time changes everything – except love. It was impossible to believe otherwise after seeing those pictures.

As I drifted into sentimentality, however, I was stopped in my tracks by a question. The same one that had come to mind after my meeting with Valérie. There was a strange parallel between the two encounters. As if both women had been trying to produce a form of narrative tension. In Valérie's case, there was no doubt about it. At the very last moment of our meeting, turning back to me to announce that she was going to leave her husband, she had clearly been attempting to create suspense. Just as every episode of a television series ends with an event that leaves the viewer eager to find out what happens next. A cliffhanger. As if writing the script of her own life, Valérie had deliberately left me with that hunger to know more. And would leave the reader in the same state, if I ever managed to write this story.

Now Madeleine was doing something similar. Not that I believed she was acting deliberately like a narrator. I found it hard to imagine her having a conscious grasp of the concept of a cliffhanger. And yet, that last scene had combined all the necessary ingredients. What was going to happen next? She wanted to see Yves again. It seemed obvious to me that I would play a role in the organisation of this reunion. Once again, it was my presence that had sparked this unexpected development in her life. I was like a psychiatrist met by chance. You speak to him without any sense that you have issues to share, yet within three minutes you have started unburdening yourself to him. In this case, though, what lay deep within Madeleine's heart was not an issue but a sort of buried treasure. While she had inevitably been knocked sideways by seeing Yves's photograph, the overpowering emotion that I had sensed in her after she had revealed her secret to me was happiness. She had never really talked to her daughters about the intensity of that first love, out of respect for their father. My book would give her the chance to tell her story at last.

Outside on the street, I walked around my neighbourhood for a while. Everywhere I looked, the people I saw were no longer residents but characters. I had often sat on café terraces and dreamed up lives for passers-by; this time, I had acted to put an end to my imaginings. Thinking about my book again, I had the feeling that it was turning into a *romance*. Between Valérie's marital crisis and Madeleine's resurrected past, my narrative was very much focused on affairs of the heart. I found this slightly annoying, as I had in the past been criticised for writing too much about love. But let's be clear: this was not my fault. I had submitted to the lives of my characters. And for most people, love was obviously one of the most important threads in the tapestry of their life.

It was almost evening already, and for the second time in two days I was going to have dinner with the Martin family. I deliberately got there a little early so I'd have time to talk to the children. Lola opened the door and greeted me with the words: 'Good evening, Mr Writer.' But that was all. She immediately returned to her bedroom, abandoning me in the hallway. Did she just not like my face? Valérie had told me the day before that her daughter was one of the popular kids at her school. All I saw was a shy teenager, as suspicious of me as if I were a surprise test in her chemistry class. This generation might have lost its capacity for surprise, but it was still well stocked with mistrust. With the rise of social media, where reputations could be built or lost on nothing at all, one had to remain vigilant. She saw me as a sort of spy, and she wasn't wrong.

I was left with no choice but to venture alone towards the living room. As I always do when invited into someone else's home, I checked out the bookshelves. I feel it's possible to find out everything about a person simply by looking at the books that they own. Back in the days when I was apartment-hunting, I would always head straight for the bookshelves to discover what novels the residents possessed. If there were none at all, I would leave immediately. I couldn't possibly have bought anything from an owner who didn't read fiction. It would have been like finding out that a horrific crime had taken place there years before. (And, yes, I know. But each to his obsessions.) Just as some people believe in ghosts, I consider it perfectly plausible that there is a sort of phantom of philistinism.

In the Martins' apartment I found a few classics, some bestsellers, and three or four Prix Goncourt winners. From a literary point of view, I was in an average family, the kind that reads the books everyone's talking about. However, I was surprised to discover a copy of Emil Cioran's *The Trouble with Being Born* in among all those mass-market paperbacks. That seemed to me as improbable as the Marx Brothers making a tragedy. But then I picked up the book and read the label stuck to it: BUY TWO, GET ONE FREE. So the Romanian philosopher had, posthumously, found himself part of a promotional offer that gave his book a fleeting glimpse of bestsellerdom. He might, I thought, have enjoyed that irony of posterity. Thinking this, I remembered one of my favourite lines by him: 'It is incredible that the prospect of having a biographer does not make anyone give up on having a life.' There was a resonance there with my own project, since I was effectively becoming the Martins' biographer.

27

Time passed and I was still alone in the living room. So I had no choice. It was time for:

INTERESTING ANECDOTES
ABOUT KARL LAGERFELD (1)[7]

Throughout his life, Lagerfeld kept some of the furniture from his childhood bedroom. That was what Madeleine had told me. I found this detail fascinating, and I am not using that word just to increase the excitement of this passage designed to fill a narrative gap. No, I find it all the more intriguing since he did not associate childhood with happiness. I remember an interview in which he said that the austere atmosphere of Michael Haneke's film *The White Ribbon* had reminded him of his own childhood. After a little more research, I also came across this Lagerfeld quote in the newspaper *Libération*: 'I found the condition of being a child humiliating.' That gives us a glimpse of what he lived through. So, of course, we have to wonder about his desire to keep belongings from the room where he lived during that period. It has been said that an artist is an adult who always looks back at his childhood, but this is different. I am

---

7. As promised, whenever I sensed a lowering of the narrative tension, or whenever my characters were not giving me what I needed to sustain the reader's interest, I would use Karl Lagerfeld.

one of those people who believe that objects carry within them vibrations of the past; just like walls, streets or trees. So the little desk that he kept throughout his life was, in a way, the first to behold his genius. It was where he made his first designs, the origin of his creative world. Lagerfeld wanted to keep close to him not the object of an era he rejected, but the material witness to his artistic birth. (The human equivalent of this would be to keep your mum with you forever.)

28

Apparently, telling a story is enough to make a story happen, because it was in the middle of this Lagerfeld anecdote that Jérémie appeared. Unlike his elusive sister, he sat down next to me. Emboldened, I asked if I could visit his bedroom. He agreed, but I quickly sensed that he was the type of person who said yes to everything in order to spare himself the bother of conversation. It was a way of saving words. And when he did speak, he never really finished his sentences; there was something incomplete about him. To be more precise: he himself did not seem very interested in what he was saying.

This is, I imagine, a fairly common condition. Adolescence is an age when one's sense of self takes a beating. A phenomenon that can perhaps be explained in this way: often, childhood is a kingdom where the child is the centre of the world. Unwittingly, parents swell their children's egos out of all proportion. They rush to meet their every need, judge every scribble a work of genius, and go into ecstasies about every ridiculous dance routine. In other words, children feel as if they are touched by grace, and their illusion is sadly shattered when they reach the truth of adolescence: they are merely themselves. Surely puberty would prove less traumatic if we were to surround humans from their earliest days with a less narcissistic reality. Jérémie, like all adolescents, was akin to a pop star who had enjoyed several big chart hits but was now going through a more complex period where the public no longer seemed interested in him. So he found himself at a stage in life when, despite not having really lived, he felt like a has-been. Adolescents think they are afraid of the future, when really they are mourning the loss of the past.

This theory went through my head as I looked around the walls of a soulless bedroom, brightened by a few posters. To judge by those posters, his musical tastes were erratic. His heart was torn between the extreme poles of Nirvana and Angèle: a band of depressives and a young woman full of *joie de vivre*. Glancing at the Nirvana poster, I asked Jérémie what he thought teen spirit smelled like. 'Like food that's gone bad,' he responded instantly. Once again, I saluted his quick wits. After that, we had a brief conversation about Kurt Cobain, and he seemed interested in what I told him: that I had been blown away by Nirvana's explosion onto the rock scene in 1991, and devastated, three years later, by their singer's suicide. I mentioned to Jérémie the famous curse of the 27 Club: the list of stars who had died at that age, including Janis Joplin, Jimi Hendrix, Jim Morrison, Brian Jones, Amy Winehouse ... But I stopped myself mid-anecdote. I did not want to win Jérémie's trust by leading him into such morbid depths. I could see it in his slightly widened eyes; he was looking at me as if I'd just offered him practical advice on how to slit his wrists.

Time to change the subject. Continuing my inspection of his room, I noted the absence of books. He had only a few classics that he'd had to read at school, such as Voltaire's *Zadig* and Stendhal's *The Red and the Black*. This surprised me: his reference to Amélie Nothomb during our first meeting had led me to imagine he was a book-lover. But that was a red herring. He explained to me that he'd never read Nothomb, but one of the girls in his class was obsessed with her. She aped the writer's fashion sense, dressing in black and wearing large hats. To create a sort of complicity between us, I told him I knew Amélie quite well – a revelation that appeared to leave him cold. He must have noticed the disappointment on my face and realised I was trying desperately to forge some connection with him, because he blurted out: 'Mbappé's the one I'd like to meet. Do you know him?' Regretfully I admitted that I had never met him. So my book was perhaps going to fail due to my lack of footballing friends. I had met Dominique Rocheteau a few years earlier, at a book fair in Saint-Étienne, and we'd talked about his experience filming with Maurice Pialat. But I doubted Jérémie would be interested in that. Time to change the subject again …

I started asking him questions about his daily life, his school, his friends. From his reactions, I had the feeling that he found me annoying. He wished he hadn't let me into his room now, I could tell. He should have done what his sister had done and simply ignored me. He answered my questions out of politeness, but most of the time his responses were vague and confused. Sometimes he would stammer out a sort of onomatopoeia; had I been Claude Lévi-Strauss, I could have spent hours dissecting his words. But I wasn't, and in the end I had to admit that I wasn't getting anything from him at all. This character was a dead end.

Even so, I continued questioning him in the hope of finding something to write about.

'So you really don't have any hobbies?' I asked casually, trying not to make it sound like an accusation.

He shrugged. 'Well, you know …'

'Um, not really. Could you explain what you mean?'

'I mean, like, I don't really have hobbies.'

'Okay … But you like music, right? Your posters … Do you like Angèle?'

'Not especially. I made some holes in the wall when I was younger, so I covered them up with posters.'

'What do you listen to?'

'Nothing comes to mind.'

'And what do you do in your spare time?'

'I play online with some mates.'

'…'

'And I like watching TV series.'

'Ah, okay. What do you watch? Could you recommend a show for me?'

'I don't know.'

'You don't know? What do you mean?'

'Nothing comes to mind.'

'…'

Apparently, TV series were just a landscape flashing past the window of his mind. Fleeting images, forgotten as soon as the next episode began. But Jérémie could surely have made a bit of an effort, come up with a name at least. Instead I had to keep posing more questions, asking him to be more specific. It was exhausting, this one-way conversation. Suddenly, to my surprise, he tried to fill the void into which our little talk had fallen.

'There's a girl at my school who tried to commit suicide.'

'Ah … that's terrible.'

'Yeah.'

'Did you know her?'

'No. Just her face.'

'Do you know what happened?'

'To start with, everyone thought she was being bullied. The teachers are always going on about that. We're supposed to tell them immediately if we see someone being picked on or whatever.'

'But that wasn't the case for this girl?'

'No. They found a letter in her bedroom.'

'And it explained why she'd done it?'

'Yeah.'

'What did it say?'

'It was really weird.'

'You don't want to tell me?'

'Yeah, but …'

'What?'

'She said it was Satan's wish. She heard a voice … the voice of the devil telling her to kill herself.'

'She wrote that in the letter?'

'Yeah.'

'Are you sure, or is that just what you heard?'

'No, I saw the letter. There's a copy going round the school. It's an incredible letter.'

'I can imagine.'

'I made a copy of it. Do you want to see?'

'Sure,' I said, trying to mask my morbid excitement. Against all the odds, an interesting and unexpected development had emerged in Jérémie's story arc. Maybe I could make a copy of the letter and put it in my book.

Jérémie went over to his desk, opened a drawer, then abruptly turned towards me.

'Did you really believe me?'

'What?'

'I invented all that. For you.'

'Why?'

'I don't know. You looked disappointed by what I was saying, so I thought it'd make you happy.'

'Make me happy? I don't know what to say … You're a surprising person. But no, I wasn't disappointed at all; I'm sorry if you thought that. I want to get to know *you*, to find out what makes you tick. How you see the world today, and the future. You don't need to invent stuff for me. Although I have to admit you did a very good job. You really had me going there.'

'Thank you.'

There was a silence. Deep down, I knew I'd made a bit of a fool of myself, churning out all those clichés about Jérémie and adolescence. Now, though, his eyes seemed to light up. Not with a big flame, just the glow of a distant candle. But it was more than I'd expected from Jérémie. A promising start.

29

An hour later, the five of us were sitting around the table, in the same configuration as the previous evening. Since they knew I'd made films, they started asking me if such-and-such an actor was a nice person. I trotted out a few well-worn truisms about each of them because I didn't want to risk revealing anyone's neuroses. We ended up trading equally dull generalisations about the weather and politics.

The Martin family often had dinner while watching television, particularly the current affairs talk show *C à vous*. Valérie was especially fond of the presenter, Anne-Élisabeth Lemoine, whom she'd met once at a flea market in Paris's fifteenth arrondissement. My presence had put paid to this relaxing ritual, forcing the family to speak to one another. Even I felt quite embarrassed by this. I didn't dare meet Patrick's eyes, lest he read in my expression the secret his wife had shared with me. I had never been very good at keeping secrets.[8] During this second evening, my project took a strange turn. I had the impression that I was in the middle of a reality TV show, minus the hysteria.

At last Patrick spoke.

'I don't mind talking to you so that you can follow our lives, as my wife has suggested, but I don't think you should have dinner with us every evening. Surely the best thing would be to meet with each of us individually.'

8. My face was an open book. Open to the page where the murderer's identity was revealed.

'Actually, I think you're right,' I said.

'Come and have lunch with me tomorrow. I'll show you where I work. You'll see it's not as nice as being a writer.'

'I'd love to. Thank you for helping me.'

'What about you, Lola?' Valérie asked her daughter, already knowing what the answer would be.

'I haven't changed my mind. I don't give a toss about being in a book. And I don't want my private life put on display like that.'

'Please don't be vulgar. Personally, I think this will be a wonderful record of our lives. Maybe people will still be talking about us a hundred years from now.'

'Well, I don't know about that,' I said, worried that she was somewhat overestimating me. 'If people are still talking about my book two weeks after it comes out, I'd be happy with that.'

'Besides, we'll be able to read the manuscript before it's published, won't we?' Valérie asked, probably to reassure her daughter.

'Sure,' I replied, while thinking that the book would lose all its interest if I had to submit it to them for approval. I was afraid that, seeing the words on paper, they would try to stop me publishing it at all. So, obviously, that was out of the question.

30

Dinner was over quickly and everyone went back to their rooms. I stayed alone with Valérie in the living room and drank herbal tea. I didn't want to bring up what she'd told me about her husband: this wasn't the time or place. I couldn't see myself whispering. And yet, one question kept gnawing at me: had her sudden declaration been spontaneous or premeditated? If the former, it was perhaps our conversation that had triggered the sharing of that secret. Would she stick to her resolution? I doubted it. It's possible to express a desire without going through with it. As I imagined my hostess's possible romantic futures, she watched me with a broad smile.

'You're really unusual.'

'Oh? Is that a compliment?'

'Yes. I love it. I did find you very odd to start with, but I have to admit that you're growing on me.'

'...'

She started laughing. Apparently she was quite pleased with what she'd said. I had known her only two days, but I had the feeling it had been a long time since she'd laughed like that. Her face seemed surprised at having to make the expressions associated with happiness and amusement. This woman who had been so withdrawn when I first met her was now clearly enjoying the idea of the adventure she'd set in motion.

She went on: 'So I didn't really understand: your wife just left you, like that?'

'She wasn't my wife.'

'You know what I mean. Your partner, then.'

'Valérie, thank you for everything. But I would really prefer not to talk about myself.'

'I know, I get it. But I need to know the person I'm talking to. And you're nothing like what they say about you on the internet.'

'I don't know what I'm like. I certainly don't want to hide from you. And I understand your desire for a greater balance in our conversations. But I'm here to write a book about you, not about me.'

'It's frustrating though. I want to get to know you better.'

'We can talk about me later, okay?'

'All right. But at least let me ask you one question a day. That's reasonable, isn't it?'

'One question a day?'

'Yes.'

'All right,' I said, smiling faintly.

At that rate, it would take her several years to understand my relationship with Marie. I had been questioning myself constantly since our separation, and I wasn't even close to finding an answer. In fact, it all seemed to be getting stranger and more uncertain; I wasn't at all sure that she and I had lived through the same experiences.

31

Having parried this autobiographical attack, I gained the upper hand again. I wanted to take advantage of this moment alone with Valérie to tell her what her mother had revealed to me. How much did Valérie know about Madeleine's first love? Not much, she said. He'd been mentioned in passing a few times; at most, she knew his first name and a few insignificant details, but she had never known how serious the relationship was. She appeared surprised by what I told her, although she did accept it was generally easier to confess one's innermost thoughts to a stranger. She had felt the same thing too, after all. But Madeleine had hidden her romantic past above all out of respect for the father of her children. And Valérie wasn't sure she wanted to know any more about it; the frown on her face was pitched somewhere between doubt and disgust. It must also be said that it was probably strange for Valérie to imagine her mother in the throes of a wild passion, when she had always seen her go about her life in such a reasonable way.

I showed her the photograph of Yves Grimbert that I had found on Facebook. She got up abruptly to fetch a bottle. 'Don't you think this calls for whisky rather than tea?' she said, in a voice that sounded almost tragic. I agreed completely.[9] It was true that I couldn't really handle hard spirits and would much

---

9. It would be possible to associate every moment of one's life with a liquid mood; there are lemonade moments and cherry vodka moments. This morning, for example, I felt quite excited by my project – very much a papaya juice mood.

rather have drunk wine. But I wanted to go along with her, to impose my own tastes on this story as little as possible. And in the end, I liked the pleasant heat that radiated through my throat; my head started to warm up nicely too, and I almost regretted all those years of drinking without a drop of whisky. A drink that propelled us towards the dark, painful part of the story. Madeleine had never known why Yves had suddenly left for the United States. Presumably he'd lacked the courage to tell her the truth, but what truth? The years had flown by, leaving her as bewildered as she had been that first day after his departure, and now here was a French writer to sweep up the crumbs of her unbroken despair.

I don't know how long our conversation lasted, but after a while Patrick came back into the living room. Well, almost: he stood in the doorway, one foot still in the corridor. He watched us, caught between stupefaction and irritation. 'You're drinking whisky?' he said finally, as he stared at the answer to his question. I accept that it could have struck him as incongruous, seeing his wife get drunk with a perfect stranger in his living room. He wanted to help me in my project, but there were limits. It was time I left.

The three of us quickly said goodbye. Out on the landing, I thought I could hear raised voices behind the door. Apparently I had outstayed my welcome and caused a marital row. I had to be careful not to disturb the equilibrium of this family; not to damage the Martins' ecosystem. By the time the lift arrived, I could no longer hear anything. That is perhaps one way to measure how worn down a couple is: when their arguments are over in a matter of seconds.

Walking home, I contemplated the richness of the day's harvest. A little earlier that day, after thinking about *Six Characters in Search of an Author*, I had found Pirandello's book in my apartment. Leafing through it, I'd come upon this phrase: 'Life is full of infinite absurdities, which, strangely enough, do not even need to appear plausible, since they are true.' Indeed, the truth often seems improbable. I was worried that my writing about reality might be considered less credible than fiction. I feared that my readers would not believe me, that they would think this entire story invented; that they would imagine I had never left my apartment and spoken to the first person I encountered. Sometimes I tell the truth and it sounds like a lie. But what can I do? Life is implausible.

I sat on the sofa in my living room for a moment. My face was warm from the alcohol, a sensation I found quite pleasant. I also remember enjoying, in that instant, the feeling of solitude that gripped me.

A few minutes later (although this interlude may have lasted longer than I realised), I stood up and went to my desk. The very desk where I was going to spend hours transforming my experiences into a book. It was obvious that I ought to note down as quickly as possible everything I saw, heard, did. I did not trust my memory.

Drumcondra Branch

Madeleine Tricot. Despite what her daughter told me about her health, she seems really quite robust and lucid regarding her past. Told me about her first love. Sounds like he was the love of her life. His name is Yves Grimbert and he lives in the United States. We looked at his photograph on Facebook. I could easily write him a message. The reasons for his departure remain mysterious. Madeleine has never stopped thinking about him. I really like this story. Will it take over my book? I also have a soft spot for René (I like shadowy, forgotten figures). A few nice anecdotes about Lagerfeld which I'm keeping up my sleeve.

Valérie Martin. Her attitude towards me has completely changed. Is now enthusiastic about my project. Seems eager to talk, but also insists on knowing more about me. I have to find a way to dodge her questions. She radiates dissatisfaction. Is no longer motivated by her job. Major revelation: she wants to leave her husband. Is this just a phase? A genuine decision? I'm afraid she's doing this to make my book more interesting.

Patrick Martin. Still somewhat suspicious of me. Nothing new today, but he did invite me to have lunch with him tomorrow. Seems totally preoccupied by his work problems, and the meeting with his boss. His jealous reaction this evening, though, makes me believe he's still in love with his wife.

Jérémie Martin. Seems to lack self-confidence —
normal for an adolescent. Made a surprising attempt
to participate in my book by telling me a completely
made-up story. I have a feeling this character could
yet surprise me.

Lola Martin. Situation unchanged. She doesn't want
me to write about her. There's no rush.

Before going to bed, I wrote to Marie: 'Do you still prefer solitude?' But I didn't send the message. I didn't feel like talking about her just then, nor did I want her to appear in my book.

The sun rose on the third day of my book. As I drank my morning coffee, I turned on my computer. I decided not to reply to the emails I'd received, to consider all external elements as a hindrance to my project. The Martin family was my religion now. I had become a devout believer, borderline intolerant towards the rest of the world. When writing, one must not let oneself be distracted by other stories. I have sometimes lost sentences by allowing my mind to wander. And there are so many temptations: one's imagination often produces parallel storylines, as if the narrator were committing adultery.

I began to shape the elements at my disposal. The colours of my characters were gradually becoming clear. After a while, however, I asked myself: am I really fascinated by this family? Or am I forcing myself to feel interested in them to prove the truth of my initial premise? Perhaps, to avoid going back on my promise to myself, I am refusing to see their banality. Perhaps I am trying to dress reality in clothes of wonder. I had felt I was on the verge of an exciting literary truth, but now I was beginning to have doubts. Then again, I was used to it. Every book I write is built around my rejection of what I'd loved the day before. I have never been blessed by certainty when I write.

That's where I was on the rollercoaster of my mind when the sound of the intercom brought it to a halt. Usually, I don't answer. When I'm writing, I play dead.[10] But I had a hunch that

10. Need to think about this phrase later.

this interruption was connected to my project. And I was right: Madeleine was waiting for me outside my apartment block. I quickly got dressed and went down to meet her. She knew I lived in this building (I'd pointed it out to her during our first encounter). She hadn't thought to ask her daughter for my phone number, but she wanted to talk to me as soon as possible. What was so urgent? I was about to ask her up for a coffee but, just as I opened my mouth, a vision of my apartment formed before my eyes. It was in too much of a mess. If she saw how I lived, she would probably back out of our budding relationship. Personally, I would never confide my most intimate secrets to someone who let dirty plates pile up in the sink. Then again, I was a writer: the perfect alibi for all forms of laxity and slovenliness. I could always tell her that, while writing, I was totally incapable of performing even the smallest practical task.

In the end we went to the café at the corner of the street. At this time of day – the mid-morning lull – the place was empty. If Madeleine had really woken with the feeling that she had to talk to me as soon as possible, she didn't seem in any particular hurry now she was sitting opposite me. There was an expression of tranquillity on her face; she looked rejuvenated. Her life had been jolted from its usual orbit, propelling her into a sort of gentle frenzy. How long had it been since she'd veered from her comfortable rut? I sensed she was enjoying this taste of adventure.

It was time for her to explain why she'd wanted to see me so urgently. She had spent most of the night thinking about our conversation, she said, and particularly about Yves's face. The fact that he could so suddenly surge up from the past had left her stunned. A name typed into a phone, and the face of her first love had appeared. I understood her perplexity. I explained to Madeleine that we'd been lucky he had a Facebook profile;

research is rarely so quick and simple. Looking through Yves Grimbert's page, however, I noticed that it hadn't been updated in just over two years. I'd sent a friend request to his page, but it had not yet been accepted. I didn't dare tell her what had already crossed my mind: that perhaps he was dead. Plenty of profiles remain active after the person's death. Even some of my own Facebook friends were deceased, and it always upset me when I received a notification reminding me to wish them a happy birthday. It is one of the small violences of contemporary life, having to unfriend an obsolete profile or delete the phone number of someone who is no longer with us.

Why had my thoughts once again taken a morbid turn, towards the worst possible version of the future? I was sitting opposite a woman filled with hope who was repeating what she'd told me the day before: 'I want to find Yves. I don't know how long I have left to live, but I can't go without seeing him one last time. Seeing him and holding him in my arms. I need to ask him why he left. Ask him if he ever thought about me during all those years. I want to see him, even for just a minute …' She spoke these words as if she'd memorised them. He lived in Los Angeles, so she would fly there as soon as possible. I could tell she was determined. The hesitant woman who'd struggled to find the right words no longer existed. I could already imagine her on that slightly crazy journey. Just then, I asked her why she'd come to see me. She replied simply: 'Since this is all your fault, I want you to come with me.'

36

I had approached a woman randomly, and two days later she wanted to travel with me to the other side of the world to track down her first love. I could hardly have hoped for a better start to my story, except maybe the confession of a crime that had haunted her conscience for decades. I was very excited by the idea of being a witness to this love story, of having a front-row seat at their reunion. I was already thinking how I would describe their faces. Perhaps all the meaning in my book would be distilled into that particular scene.

Of course, all this remained hypothetical for now. I'd still not heard back from Yves. If he didn't accept my friend request, I would go ahead and send him a message anyway. But if that happened, there was a chance he wouldn't read it. I lost myself in these modern misgivings, without being sure that I truly understood them. I had never been a big fan of technology, and I had generally kept my distance from social media, afraid that it would eat up my time. For a curiosity junkie, social media was a bottomless pit of temptation. I didn't mind having a Facebook account, because its popularity was declining as Instagram rose. I had also looked Yves Grimbert up on Google, but had found nothing. It struck me as surprising that anyone could slip through the (inter)net without a trace. I'd found a few people with the same name, but none in Los Angeles.

Although I wasn't sure it would come to anything, I had to talk to Valérie about her mother's plan. No doubt she would be opposed to Madeleine making such a trip. A time comes when the children become their parents' parents, when they start to decide what is acceptable or not in their elders' lives. But Madeleine, I felt sure, would go with or without her daughter's blessing. I could sense a new certainty within her, driving her forward.

37

In the meantime, I had to meet Patrick for lunch. My schedule had rarely been this full, and never before had I had so many meetings, back to back, with members of the same family – not even my own. This was my version of Pasolini's *Theorem*, minus the perversion and the sexual relations. I didn't think I had much in common with Patrick, and that suited me in a way. I thought it would be interesting to confront a character who was potentially hostile to my project or who didn't like me very much.

He greeted me with a bare minimum of politeness. Presumably he'd agreed to speak to me to make his wife happy; he was in that period of life when it seemed simpler to give in. As with Valérie, he chose to meet me in a restaurant close to his workplace. I was disappointed; I'd imagined being given the grand tour of the insurance company, having lunch in the staff canteen. I was fascinated by that life. When I went to secondary schools to talk to the students about my books, I always asked for a school dinner. To me, egg mayonnaise served in a small plastic bowl was the height of gastronomic pleasure.

Above all, though, I would have liked to observe him in his professional environment to better understand him. After lunch, perhaps he could take me up to his office on the fourteenth floor. Although, as Patrick had explained: 'Technically, I'm on the thirteenth floor, but since that's an unlucky number, there is no thirteenth floor. It seems absurd to me, because what you call it makes no difference to the curse. If you're superstitious, you know perfectly well you're on the thirteenth floor, even if it's marked fourteen on the lift button.' I wasn't sure how to respond to this remark, which seemed to me full of common sense, so I simply nodded to communicate my absolute agreement.

38

A few minutes later, we were sitting in an Italian restaurant, which offered a set lunch deal. Patrick opted for that without really looking at the details. The check paper napkins and the unlit candles gave the place a vague suggestion of romance, providing an unlikely atmosphere for our meeting. The man sitting opposite me was clearly making an effort to do his social duty; he had no real desire to talk to me. But I wasn't going to waste time beating around the bush, so I remarked that he did not appear particularly enthusiastic about life, indeed that he was going through a very difficult period. To be more specific, what I actually said was:

'Things seem tough right now.'

'Yeah.'

'And from what you said yesterday, it's obviously getting to you.'

'Yeah.'

'I don't want to bother you with my project, but I'd really like it if we could talk about this. About how you feel, what you're going through. I have the impression that you're not very happy.'

He sat there in silence, as if dumbstruck. I, a stranger, was passing judgement on his existence. And he hadn't even asked my opinion. I'd made a very bad start. I should have begun with a memory of better times, something to lift him from his gloom. I thought he was about to get up and leave, but instead he started talking. It was true, he said: this was a difficult time, and he didn't know how to extricate himself from this downward spiral.

'You're a victim of bullying,' I said compassionately, in part to compensate for my earlier abrupt tone. He seemed surprised that this label could be attached to the chaos he was enduring. He said he personally was not a victim, but that the current restructuring was causing problems. The arrival of the new managing director, Desjoyaux, had plunged the entire company into hell. Patrick repeated almost word for word what he'd told me during our first dinner; the familiar refrain of his distress. So, sensing that he needed to escape the present, I asked him how things had been before.

As he began to talk about what sounded in retrospect like a golden age, some colour returned to his face. At the start of his career, everything had seemed possible. As a salesman, he would travel almost every day to visit his clients. His life felt intense, frenetic, even if he was just going to talk to a dentist in some godforsaken suburb. He loved his job and he felt useful: selling insurance was not an attempt at extortion but a genuine effort to protect people from potential risk. With only the slightest hint of exaggeration, he saw himself as a sort of saviour in waiting. Whenever he signed a contract, he felt a shiver run down his spine. He was so successful that he ended up becoming a manager: a promotion he couldn't refuse, but that left a bitter aftertaste. Was it possible for professional progress to be experienced as a personal setback? He missed his travelling days. When he used to be greeted with: 'Ah, Monsieur Martin, would you like some coffee?' Or, if it was the last meeting of the day: 'I'm not going to let you leave without having a drink. I've got a very nice Juliénas, and you can tell me all your news ...' He yearned for those small moments of pleasure with clients. There was nothing exciting about the hours he spent analysing statistics. He had sometimes considered a change of direction, but where would he go? It was this that scared him most, the idea that there was no alternative.

Of course, his work life was not completely devoid of pleasure. It was wonderful to have played a part in his company's rise. And he felt satisfaction at doing his job well. To him, that was very important. Back in his school days, Patrick had always been a good student.[11]

Since the 2008 financial crisis, a number of things had changed. The company had lost money, which had led to redundancies, and that in turn had led to increasingly onerous demands on the remaining employees. Patrick's career had been upended by a succession of restructuring plans, in which less and less attention was paid to the needs of the people who worked for the company. And then a new managing director had arrived: Jean-Paul Desjoyaux. A tall, thin man who might have been sculpted by Giacometti, although he was obviously less pleasing to the eye than a work by the Swiss sculptor. As soon as he arrived, he gave his employees a strange order: they must never speak to him unless he spoke to them first. Some had thought this was just a rumour, but it turned out to be true. In any case, nobody dared to contradict this new diktat. So when you passed him in a corridor, you were forbidden to say hello unless he said hello to you. On days when he didn't wish to be encumbered with polite conversation, he was able to walk through the entire office in complete silence. On the other hand, as soon as he did address someone, that person was expected to respond immediately. It was very much a one-way relationship. This situation quietly left the employees in a state of permanent anxiety; when they passed Desjoyaux, they never knew – until the last moment – if they would have to speak or remain silent. Some forms of torture can appear perfectly harmless.

---

11. Not only that, but he'd also always been a good son, a good citizen, a good husband, a good father. In other words, he ticked every box for a man who was about to explode.

Patrick returned to the subject of his summons. 'Seventy-two hours of torment,' he said openly. Seventy-two hours before he knew what Desjoyaux wanted from him. Perhaps he was about to be fired. He'd been anticipating that, unlike some of his colleagues, who'd been shocked to discover they had lost their jobs. He was thinking in particular of Gerbier, who'd spent three months in a daze in his bedroom. This was the second time, after Lambert, that Patrick had mentioned the post-job trajectory of a sacked colleague. Patrick would regularly call Gerbier's wife to find out how he was, but the news never seemed to improve. This man who had always been so cheerful and full of life was now vegetating in bed. He didn't want to go out any more, didn't want to see anyone. Not even his own children. He had become convinced that he was useless. Patrick didn't think Gerbier would have the courage to kill himself, but then he was already dead in a sense. The incessant humiliations had knocked him off his feet, transformed him from a man into a shadow. Patrick didn't know what he could do to help him, other than those calls to his wife, a reminder of his presence – even if it was only that of a disembodied voice.

The example of Gerbier had enabled him to anticipate his own dismissal. So he'd prepared psychologically, as they say. Although the expression is not wholly convincing, since it is difficult to gauge the effects of a situation until you have actually lived through it. In any case, Patrick had attempted to visualise that other life. With his experience, he would surely be able to find a new job. But that would take time; offers of work at his level were rare. Obviously this would bring financial worries, but there was something else that haunted him: how would he fill those weeks or months of nothingness? He was used to the demands of time management, but not when he had no work with which to fill that time. Patrick had asked himself questions: did he have any hobbies? He had the impression that the accumulated stress of the past few years had left him an empty husk. He no longer felt any desire at all. So, the answer was no: he had no real hobbies. He didn't want to watch films or read books or visit museums or go for walks or travel the world or play a new sport ... He imagined wandering through long empty days like a soldier in search of a war. While he waited for the fateful meeting with Desjoyaux, he found himself obsessed by the image of those endless hours.

39

The years passed but something was missing. Patrick and I were the same age, so we could understand each other. When you reach your mid forties, you are too old to be young. But you are still a bit too young to be old. You navigate your existence through an uncomfortable in-between zone. Patrick thought about all the years he had spent fulfilling his destiny: creating a family, forging a career. But what remained of all that? Teenage children who would soon fly the nest, a stale marriage, and a car crash of a career. I understood how he felt. I muttered a few suitable phrases about the human capacity to bounce back, about the fact that nobody was dying. But every time I tried to console him, he repeated wearily: 'Yeah, that's easy for you to say ...'[12] He imagined my life as a kingdom without borders, free of all difficulties. I didn't react to this because I had no desire to talk about myself, but I did give my opinion on his situation.

'You don't have to let this sink you. You've had a brilliant career. I'm sure you can find another job. You have plenty of transferable skills ...'

'It's obvious you don't live in the real world. I have debts to pay off, I have to send my kids to university, I have to help my parents. And there are always bills that need paying.'

'...'

'Can you tell me why all kids have crooked teeth and why they

12. He was calling me *tu* by this point; we had left the more formal *vous* behind just before the arrival of the aubergines au gratin.

all need expensive dental work? None of that existed when we were young.'

'Yeah, but look at our teeth,' I said, trying to lighten the mood.

'Do you even understand what I'm saying? I feel so much pressure. It's suffocating me. So, yeah, it's easy to say I could just change my life. Maybe in your world I could, but not in mine.'

'I'm just saying you could try to be a bit positive. You shouldn't just forget everything you've achieved.'

'Yeah ... I suppose you're right,' he admitted, as the waiter brought him his *île flottante*: a meringue island floating in a sea of vanilla custard.

He stared at his dessert for a moment without speaking, but I could see a spark of joy light up his eyes. Yes, that floating island had illuminated something inside him for the first time since we had begun talking. You know things are bad when your only consolation comes in the form of pudding. He looked as lost as a child, no longer fully capable of making adult decisions. I felt for this man, whom I had judged too quickly. He was all at sea professionally, and of course that had spilled over into his married life. Valérie had spoken so harshly about him. Had she meant what she said? I found myself wanting to vaunt Patrick's qualities to his wife, to plead mitigating circumstances, but was that my role? I was there to write a book, not to become a sort of mediator. But by meddling like this in a family's life, I had ended up at the intersection of all its problems. I had a panoramic view of the situation. I could hear all the false notes in their dissonant orchestra.

True, their marriage was in crisis. But let's be honest, who isn't in crisis? Life is a series of crises, whether individual (adolescence, midlife, existential) or collective (financial, moral, epidemiological). And that's without even mentioning the bodily manifestations (liver, nerves, etc.). In the western world, crisis has become an all-purpose slogan. Essentially, it comes down to the absolute loneliness of each individual. I often think about the famous quotation by Albert Cohen: 'Every man is alone and no one gives a damn about anyone and our sorrows are a desert island.' Let us at least hope that it is a floating island.

40

Yet again, I had to be careful not to get too involved. I wasn't there to give my opinion, but to write about these people's lives. I had to keep him talking, even if it made him feel worse.

As Patrick savoured his dessert, lingering over it to prolong the pleasure, I asked about his love life. He looked up at me and I sensed his hesitation: did he want to answer that question? Probably not. He was very much a modest man, the kind who doesn't confide in others, not even his closest friends. He decided to turn the question on me.

'What about you – what was your longest relationship?'

'Me? I'd say … seven years,' I replied, uncertain how long the relationship in question had actually lasted, since there had been several separations within it, little interludes, but overall I did think that, measured end to end, our relationship had endured approximately that long.

'So you can't understand.'

'Why?'

'Living twenty-five years with the same person is pure fiction for you.'

He wasn't wrong about that. Although I felt I'd experienced the weariness and complexity of a long-term relationship, I couldn't imagine how it would feel after spending so long with someone. I sensed from the look on his face that he was judging my love life in the light of my profession. It was typical of an artist, he seemed to be thinking, to have a series of lovers. Unsatisfied with this single cliché, he tried out some others. I didn't dare tell him that, to my mind, he was the artist. To spend so long with one person, you must surely be an accomplished actor. (See, I can be sarcastic too.)

'For all your undoubted talent, I don't think you can imagine what I'm going through,' he said.

'But that's the whole point of my project. Trying to understand the essence of a reality that isn't mine.'

'Why don't you write about yourself? All writers do that.'

'It doesn't interest me.'

'And you think what I have to say is more interesting?'

'Yes. You just said it yourself. I can't know what it's like to be in a long marriage. So tell me.'

Patrick looked at his watch; he had to get back to work. But he could see that I didn't want him to leave me like that, on the shores of his marital confession. In the end he said he would inform the office he had a meeting with a client, so he could keep talking to me. I think the truth is that he wanted to talk; he wanted me to believe that he was doing me a favour, but in reality he was doing it for himself. He began by lowering my expectations: 'I don't think there's anything to say really. It's all pretty classic. Basically, the problem is the body. Yep, that's the crux of the problem. In any relationship, there comes a time when something very strange, something terrible happens. You make love without wanting to. You make love out of a sense of duty, because you feel obliged to show that you still desire the other person. I remember that moment quite vividly. I was tired, I wanted to sleep, but I could see in Valérie's eyes that she was thinking: another night without sex. I couldn't even remember the last time we'd done it. We had two children, we lived together all the time; the desire had faded. So we found ourselves pretending. We wondered what other people did. Did they lie, did they cheat on each other, did they take pills? Valérie wanted us to talk to someone. A sort of counsellor who would help us want each other again. I thought it was a stupid idea, but I went along with it. I wanted to show that I was trying. But there was nothing to say. Life is badly designed, that's just how it is. Either you get used to the lack of desire or you split up. But we got along perfectly well; there was no reason to split up. We agreed about the children's education, we saw things the same way, we hardly ever argued. At one point, I even thought that was maybe the problem. It would have been easier to hate each other or tear each other to pieces. But we were like a drowning couple who held hands instead of trying to swim. I thought about having an affair, but I didn't feel capable of that. I didn't feel any disapproval for some of my friends who cheated on their wives. Everyone does what he can with his desire. But I couldn't do that. I don't think it even had anything to do with love. I just felt that if I went with another woman, I would be destroying what we had. And I didn't want that. I still don't want that. I know we don't show each other enough affection, I know I don't have enough energy for her, but I couldn't live without Valérie. I need her presence. Even if we don't talk, I know she's there. But I can tell she's upset with me, I can tell she's not happy any more. She's always criticising me for being lethargic, for never organising anything, for not making decisions any more. I know all that, but it's this weight on my shoulders that's holding me down. For a long time, I thought the storm would pass, that we would come out the other side and there'd be better days ahead, but it's like we've been sucked into this downward spiral. And it's so hard to climb back up to happiness. I don't know what to do to change things …'

I wanted to say: 'Tell her all this! Tell her exactly what you just told me!' But I sensed he wasn't capable of it. Often, the most beautiful declarations are made to the wrong ears. Our conversation was over; he had to get back to work. Outside the restaurant we shook hands, almost like friends. He walked a few yards, then turned back to me. Just like Valérie had done before she announced that she wanted to leave him. He turned back to tell me: 'You know, I love Valérie. I really love her.'

41

Patrick saw the situation with perfect clarity. Some of the words he'd used were identical to those used by his wife. They shared the same view of their daily life; the only difference was that Valérie wanted it to end. However, I was still waiting to see her again so she could reiterate her intention. Just as I was thinking about her, she sent me a message asking how my lunch meeting with her husband had gone. I wanted to reply: 'You'll read about it in the book.' After all, I didn't have to tell each person what the other was saying about them. There was a form of professional secrecy involved in what I was doing. But I guessed that what she really wanted to know was whether he'd been cooperative. So I replied that he was perfectly charming.

Perhaps, in the end, I would be the architect of a rapprochement between the two of them. But I had to be careful not to let their worries and sadnesses infect me. I was surely too sensitive to be a sort of blotting paper for other people's suffering. I wondered how doctors and psychiatrists managed it, how they shielded themselves from the painful confessions, the tragic lives of their patients. Would I have to be like an actor, hanging up my character in the theatre dressing room before going home? I had to observe the Martin family while attempting to feel as little empathy for them as possible; I needed a cold, clinical narrative distance from them, a buffer zone. But I couldn't write like that. It was impossible to prevent myself feeling anything about the subject of my book.

I had been genuinely surprised by Patrick's attitude. He hadn't just played along, he'd been open and sincere, particularly where his love life was concerned. He had told me everything, even ending with a declaration of love. Of course, I suspected that his words were ultimately intended for his wife; when she read my book, she would understand many things about him. But that had not been his only motivation. That afternoon, he'd sent me a message: 'I hope you have everything you need. I actually enjoyed talking to you. Good luck with your book.' It was clear from this that the conversation we'd just had was to be our last. He had told me everything because he wanted to get it over with. He had agreed to take part in my project, and he'd provided me with enough material to make him a character in the book, but he did not want me to become part of his daily life. Valérie would confirm this to me that evening.

It was a frustrating situation. I wanted to get to know him better. And I wanted to know, for example, what would happen at his meeting with Desjoyaux. I hated the idea of leaving certain storylines unfinished. Valérie reassured me on this point: she would keep me in the loop. She would help me write the rest of her husband's story. This was satisfactory from a narrative point of view (I wouldn't miss any twists or turns in Patrick's story), but not from an emotional point of view (I would find out about him only through the prism of his wife). But that was how it was: I would just have to go along with my characters' wishes. This was the major difference with fiction. In a novel, I could force anyone to tell me anything.

42

I was supposed to meet Valérie at eight that evening. We were going out to dinner. She'd mentioned a restaurant near their home that she really liked. But then, in her last message, she added: 'Could you come to the apartment first? Jérémie would like to see you.' I was intrigued by this. Was he going to reveal some secret or hidden feeling? It was also pleasing in terms of the book's age balance. With Madeleine having such an important storyline, I would need a teenager to provide a counterpoint. I always see the books I write as cocktails, in which the various ingredients must be perfectly dosed to achieve the desired result. In geometric terms, every novel has a shape – and I like mine to be round.

I decided to go home before my meeting with Jérémie. I wanted to note down what Patrick had told me, but I felt exhausted. Listening to others requires unwavering attention, and it's much more tiring than talking. Surprisingly, I managed to take a twenty-minute nap – an unusual achievement for me, as my relationship with sleep is jittery and unstable. During that short nap, I had a strange dream: Milan Kundera came up to me and whispered something in my ear, but I didn't catch what he said. In my dream, his expression was very serious, as though he were about to reveal his most precious secret to me. But I heard nothing at all. I woke up with a feeling of despair at that silence; the dream had felt so real. I had been lucky enough to meet the great Czech writer before, and he had even called me on the phone – the greatest moment in the life of my ears. But why hadn't I heard anything in my dream? Not a word, not a sigh. I really wished he could help guide me through the labyrinth of commas.

I lay there for a short while in that Kunderian atmosphere before going over to my computer. I logged into my Facebook account. I'd received a few messages, but I didn't reply to them. At the risk of seeming impolite or ungrateful, I had to remain focused on my project. Over the years, I'd succeeded in acquiring a sense of detachment towards what people thought of me. It was a relief not to feel that incessant pressure of others' judgement any more. As I was thinking this, however, I noticed that Yves Grimbert had accepted my friend request. I don't know why I hadn't noticed it before, but as soon as I did I felt a surge of excitement, as if he were my own lost lover. I thought about the girls I had loved during my childhood – Cécile Bleicher and Célia Bouet – and I practically started trembling. I had to write to him, but what should I write? I didn't know how to find the words. I was the spokesman for a love affair that I knew almost nothing about. I decided to keep it simple, to stick to the facts. I was a friend of Madeleine's, and she would be happy to see him again. There, that was enough. Regards. No, too cold. Best wishes. Yes, that was better. And, with a click, the message was sent.

I sat there staring at the page. My message had been read instantly. Sitting in my chair in the living room, I felt as if I were in the middle of an action film. I had to stay calm; it might not be him at all; it could be someone else who looked after his account, one of his children, for example. I drifted back into negative thoughts. No, stay positive! Until this point, everything had gone swimmingly with my book. There was no reason why that should change now. Oh! Three little dots had begun to flash up on the screen. That meant he was replying. Was Yves Grimbert himself writing something at that very moment? What time was it in Los Angeles? There was a nine-hour time difference. So that meant it was 7.30 a.m. there. I immediately imagined him with his coffee in the kitchen, replying to my message. Or perhaps he was in bed with his phone? No, I didn't believe that. Old people in the United States get up early; they do everything early, in fact; they have dinner around five in the afternoon. Why was I thinking about American seniors' mealtime habits? I was just filling the interminable waiting time while those three little dots quivered before my eyes. Facebook must have invented those dots to keep us hanging on; to keep the user in suspense; to let the recipient prepare himself for the coming message like an actor rehearsing his lines backstage; to prevent the connection ever being broken … yes, that was it: *never break the connection*. Even the silences between responses have become part of our entertainment; something is always happening now, even when nothing is happening.

At last his reply appeared: 'Dear Monsieur, I was very moved to read your message. In fact, it is a shock for me to hear about Madeleine this morning. I think about her so often. Please send her my most faithful thoughts. And tell her that I would be more than happy to see her again. It has been a long time since I travelled back to France. But if she would like to come here, I would be delighted. Thank you once again for sending this message on her behalf. Best wishes, Yves.'

So now it was official: I had a new character in my book. And what an elegant entrance he had made! Already, I wanted to know everything about him. Who was he? What did he do? And why had he left France? I was thinking about my book, of course, but I was also thinking about Madeleine. She would surely be overwhelmed with emotion when she read his message. People often talk about the power of literature. But it was crazy to think how many aspects of the Martins' lives had suddenly turned into gripping storylines since I'd made the decision to write about them.

43

Before meeting Jérémie, I went to Madeleine's apartment to announce the news. She did not seem surprised. For her, everything had been clear since that morning. She had not imagined any other scenario. I was fascinated by the power of her conviction. And by her pragmatism too. She handed me her passport and asked if I could book the flights. I had become her private secretary on this voyage into her past. I had a sudden intuition that something awaited me too in Los Angeles. But what it could be, I had no idea.

Madeleine couldn't help offering me tea; it was a sort of ritual for her. As we sat peacefully together, she said: 'When I left you this morning, I thought we would never see each other again.'

'Really?' I asked. 'Why ever not?'

'You have better things to do than accompany me to the other side of the world.'

'On the contrary: that trip is the most exciting part of my project.'

'You really think so?'

'Yes.'

'And your readers too?'

'No one ever knows what will interest a reader. Maybe some of them will skip all the pages about the trip to America. But I'm sure that anyone who's had regrets in life will relate to your desire to find that man again.'

'Everybody has regrets, don't they?'

'Well, there you are: that's a good sign. We'll have all the depressed people on our side, and that's a *lot* of people.'

Madeleine did not smile at this. There was a new seriousness about her. Her words had surprised me. How could she possibly have imagined that I wouldn't want to go with her? She must have thought that my initial approach to her had been a sort of whim, and that she shouldn't expect this fairy-tale-like turn in her life to continue. Well, she was wrong. Rarely had I felt so passionate about a story. I could only hail the triumph of reality. It also surprised me that Madeleine, like all my other characters, seemed so worried about whether her life would interest my readers. It was as if my publishers' marketing director had infiltrated their minds.

I reassured them all, but in truth I had no idea what would be interesting or not for a reader. I remember a journalist who'd written a review of the first of my books to reach a wide readership: 'This book works because it contains all the ingredients of success!' What a strange phrase. If I'd known the ingredients of success, I would have used the recipe earlier in my career – and spared myself all those years of doing other jobs to subsidise my writing. Besides, if the ingredients of success really did exist, everyone would be able to effortlessly produce bestsellers. It was absurd. You never really know what readers will like. Reading these lines that I'm writing now, some readers will perhaps be captivated while others will be yawning with boredom. That is not my priority. Not that I am unconcerned about the reader, but what drives me above all is feeling an obsessive passion for my subject.

But I was prepared to make compromises to reassure my characters. To try to captivate the reader, I could always rely on a few tricks. I could ask you, reader, to take part in the next stage of the book. You could try, for example, to work out why Yves

Grimbert had left Madeleine. That would make the story more fun and give it an obvious popular appeal.

POSSIBLE REASONS

FOR YVES GRIMBERT'S DEPARTURE

— He had a false identity. And the secret services were about to unmask him.

— An incurable disease. He decided to leave rather than make the woman he loved watch him die.

— He loved another woman.

— He loved another man.

— He was involved in a crime and risked being sent to prison.

— He had a double life in the United States.

— He was a nihilist and, knowing that all stories must have an end, he preferred, as Serge Gainsbourg wrote, to *flee happiness out of fear it will disappear*.

— He couldn't stand living in France any more.

— He discovered that Madeleine was in fact his sister.

— He won the lottery, but didn't want to share the prize money.

As for myself, I did have a vague hunch, but I preferred not to share it in case I influenced anyone.

44

I brought an end to this internal digression and returned to concrete reality. I asked Madeleine how much money she had for her trip. She mentioned the fact that this might be her last ever long journey. So she wanted to enjoy herself. In fact, she wanted *us* to enjoy *our*selves, so she insisted on paying for my plane ticket. After all, I was accompanying her, she said, and she wanted to thank me. I replied that I had my own reasons for going, that I was hoping her reunion would provide my book with a climactic emotional moment, but it made no difference: she was going to pay for our flights. She agreed, on the other hand, that I could take care of the hotel rooms and the car rental. Yes, I know, such details might seem superfluous, but once I have firmly grasped reality, I can't just gloss over the technical aspects. When I see certain films, I find myself wondering how the characters manage to pay for apartments that appear out of their price range; I find I can't suspend disbelief in a story if it is completely disconnected from material truth. So I thought it necessary, in terms of this book's credibility, that I should include this conversation.

Watched by Madeleine, I booked the flights on my phone. I also applied for visas. 'We leave in three days,' I told her. I could see the thrilled amazement in her eyes; for years, her whole life had been planned in advance, and even the shortest trip would be booked months ahead. It is the *death of the unexpected* that marks the true turning point of a life, the descent into old age.

The imminence of our departure made me think about Marie. The journey itself is, for me, the best part of any holiday; you can visit the world's most beautiful monuments, experience rare and intense moments, but nothing beats sitting next to your companion on a train or a plane. I remembered one flight to Asia when Marie and I had talked uninterruptedly for hours. We held hands as the plane experienced turbulence, and never before had I felt so happy.

That thought plunged me into a state of melancholy. We should be able to prevent memories flashing into our heads like that, to block them at the doorway of the present. Yet another skill we have not mastered. It should also be said that certain elements of the present contain unbearable echoes of the past. I would never be able to take a plane again without thinking of Marie.[13] But Madeleine and Yves's story resonated with me in other ways. I, too, had been dumped without understanding why. True, there had been a few post-mortem discussions ('I prefer solitude to you'), but not enough to explain the death of our love. The one who leaves the other should always provide hundreds of pages clearly setting out their reasons. They should write a thesis attempting to justify an act that the other will never understand. I felt close to Madeleine, and to her bewilderment. So often we probe into the lives of others seeking clues to explain our own life.

---

13. In the same way, I can never hear a Souchon song without thinking about sushi.

Maybe I shouldn't have said yes to everything. Seeing Jérémie before having dinner with Valérie struck me as a somewhat hectic evening. Of course, after asking the members of a family to speak to me, I did feel a certain obligation to make myself available to them. It was my duty to submit to their will, to live in the dictatorship of their reality. But I was afraid that my powers of concentration would let me down; after a certain point, I knew, my brain started to resemble the Soviet Union in 1989. Would I be capable of making the most of the information I was going to receive? Given what was about to happen with Jérémie, my fears were probably justified.

And yet things started well. He greeted me with a big smile, looking almost relieved. I assumed he was about to take the place I'd assigned him in my book, no doubt prompted by his parents. He began by asking politely: 'So how's your project going?'

'Pretty well, thanks. I'm going to the United States with your grandmother.'

'Oh, really? Why?'

'She wants to see someone who lives there.'

'Who?'

'A man she used to love. Before she met your grandfather.'

'Seriously? That's too weird.'

'Weird? I don't know about that. I think it will be very emotional for her.'

'And you're going to talk about all that in your book?'

'Well, I need to see how it goes first, but probably.'

'Cool.'

'So … You wanted to see me? I was very pleased when your mother told me that. Like I told you, it's important for me that you're in my book.'

'Oh yeah … But …'

'What?'

'It wasn't just for the book. Well, I mean, kind of … Because we can talk and that. But I wanted to see you for something else too.'

'Okay …'

'Well, it's just that I have this French homework to hand in tomorrow, and to be honest I don't understand it at all, so I thought maybe you could help me out.'

'…'

I was speechless. He must have seen that I was hoping for something else altogether when I came to see him. The disappointment was written all over my face. He hadn't wanted a novelist, but a private tutor. Then again, maybe this was a good way of forging a connection with him. The intimate conversation could come afterwards, lying in ambush behind the essay-writing advice.

When he showed me the text he had to analyse, however, I immediately realised this was not going to be easy. It was François Villon's 'La Ballade des pendus'. I have to admit that I've never been a huge fan of medieval poetry. I had some excellent teachers when I was at school, and some of them helped influence my love of words, but I doubt any teenager can be encouraged to feel enthusiastic about a poem in Old French. I didn't want to say any of this to Jérémie, of course, since that would only discourage him. So instead I exaggerated my excitement, going on about how I adored this particular poem. He didn't look very convinced. And who could blame him? I was speaking like an actor at an audition, about to hear the dread words: 'We'll call you.'

These are the opening lines of the poem:

> *O brother men who after us remain,*
> *Do not look coldly on the scene you view,*
> *For if you pity wretchedness and pain,*
> *God will the more incline to pity you.*
> *You see us hang here, half a dozen who*
> *Indulged the flesh in every liberty*
> *Till it was pecked and rotted, as you see,*
> *And these our bones to dust and ashes fall.*
> *Let no one mock our sorry company,*
> *But pray to God that He forgive us all.*

First of all, I looked at the French textbook to refresh my memory. I read that François Villon had written this poem in prison, while thinking that he might be sentenced to death. I could always start by dramatising the story behind the poem.

'You have to think about this poem ... as if he wrote it imagining it would be the last thing he ever wrote. Look at the lexical field.'

'The what?'

'The lexical field. It's a way of grouping different words belonging to the same family ... You don't notice all the violent images?'

'Yeah, I suppose so. Like "pecked" and "rotted", you mean?'

'Exactly. That's a clue. What does it make you think of?'

'Rotted? I dunno ... rotten fruit?'

'Yeah, sure. But what else?'

'A decomposing body.'

'There you go. Very good.'

'That's gross. I don't get why Martinez is making us read this.'

INTERESTING ANECDOTES
ABOUT KARL LAGERFELD (2)

His mother was an austere woman. Madeleine told me she'd seen Frau Lagerfeld one day in the Chanel offices; she was a very old woman by then. And Karl had whispered to her: 'My mother was always that old ...' Beyond his sarcasm, it was clear that he loved and admired his mother, despite the emotional distance she kept from him. She was so severe-looking that you'd assume she was a very logical person, but she had a sort of secret addiction: she consulted fortune tellers. In the summer of 1939, she summoned one of these women to their home. Seeing young Karl, she put her finger to her lips. But he was used to that. Silence was his mother's favourite melody. How old would he have been at the time? No one really knows. Karl never revealed his date of birth. Maybe four or five. Anyway, he sat in a corner of the living room and watched the scene unfold. He was amazed to see that his mother looked suddenly like a little girl in the presence of this clairvoyant and her cards. After a while, the two women turned to look at him. Had he sighed too loudly? No. He'd even learned to breathe without the air leaving his lungs. They were simply talking about him. Later, Karl would find out what they'd been saying. His mother had asked the fortune teller: 'What will my little boy become?' The fortune teller had closed her eyes, as if the contours of the future were more easily visible in the dark, before confidently announcing: 'A priest!' Lagerfeld's mother had almost fainted. She may have been a believer, but she found it inconceivable that her son would devote his life to God. She did not like this prediction at all. So she decided to change it: sometimes people see fortune tellers not to find out what the future will bring but to alter it. From that moment on, young Karl never set foot in a church again. His mother even banned him from attending family weddings and funerals. Oddly, despite pursuing a career as far from the priesthood as could be imagined, he led a relatively monastic life, often dressing in a style quite close to that of a man of the cloth.

Sorry, I had to press the Karl Lagerfeld button. I couldn't possibly let my book be weighed down by a commentary on a poem by François Villon. At this point in my story, it would have been too much of a risk. Particularly since my feeble attempts at literary analysis went on for a good hour. Jérémie looked dubious. I fully understood his surprise and disappointment. How could a professional writer have such a shaky grasp of the history of literature? How could he not know exactly what his colleagues were thinking? To him, I was like a professional footballer who had turned up on the local pitch and seemed incapable of kicking a ball. I tried to explain to him that it was possible to write without necessarily being a literary theorist. In fact, it was even possible to write a masterpiece without having any literary culture at all. But clearly Jérémie's image of a writer was the conventional one: a man living in an attic surrounded by encyclopaedias. Maybe I should just have been honest. Maybe I should have admitted that I was pretty clueless when it came to Old French. I wasn't sure what attitude to adopt with him.

At last Valérie came home, bringing my torture to an end. I

left Jérémie's bedroom feeling even more put out since I hadn't managed to gather any information that would enable me to shed new light on his character. But I had to take my time and not lose heart. My project required a level of patience that didn't come naturally to me. In truth, all of us lack patience these days. By permitting us to get what we want at the swipe of a screen, by putting us permanently in touch with others, this age is teaching us impatience. Just as we do yoga to relax, we should perhaps practise waiting. To help others, we should systematically arrive late for all our meetings.

And in fact, Valérie did ask me to wait while she got ready to go out. Sitting alone in the living room, I had the impression that I had gone back in time, to when I first arrived. Just then, Lola walked through the room, graciously offering me a brief nod. Our relationship, too, was going backwards: now I was no longer even granted the sound of her voice. But I did notice one interesting detail about her: she had no aptitude for announcing her appearances. In other words, she was the kind of character who enters a room *suddenly*. This made me think of Stavrogin, the hero of Dostoyevsky's *Demons*. At one point, the narrator says of this character that he enters a salon, having already begun talking in the corridor. As with Lola, there was a sort of humiliation to be found in transitions.

I had barely formed this thought when it was confirmed: Lola suddenly appeared in front of me. As if she'd dropped from the ceiling. She stared into my eyes for a moment, incredibly deep into my eyes, before murmuring: 'Since everyone here is talking to you, I thought I may as well do it too. So here's the situation: I'm in love with a boy. His name is Clément and he's a year older than me. We've been seeing each other for the past month. And it's going really well. But things are getting hotter between us. He wants us to have sex. And I'm not sure. Because he's already had sex with four or five girls at my school. Everyone knows it. And after that, it's over. So, basically, part of me is afraid that he'll dump me as soon as he gets what he wants. And another part thinks he's the one I want to lose my virginity with, no matter what happens afterwards. What do you think?'

I didn't have time to react. Valérie entered the living room just then and announced almost cheerfully: 'I'm ready!' Then she looked at us and asked: 'What are you two talking about?'

'We have little secrets too,' said Lola.

'I thought you didn't want to be in the book.'

'I changed my mind. Anyway, I'll leave you to it ...'

Lola left the room without a backward glance, saddling me with her problem. At first, I'd thought she was pulling my leg. But then she came back and handed me a piece of paper with this Clément guy's phone number on it, speaking in a whisper so her mother wouldn't hear. She wanted me to call him to find out what his intentions were. Again, I didn't know whether to take her seriously. The whole thing seemed rather twisted.

In the middle of the living room, Valérie stood in front of me. She was obviously expecting me to say something about her appearance. She was wearing make-up and her body was sheathed in a skin-tight dress, elevated on high heels; her outfit was a trailer for the film of her thoughts. By the looks of it, this was to be more a romantic date than a professional interview. And, although I couldn't deny that she looked radiant, I was obviously in an embarrassing position. All of this seemed beside the point. I was there to write a book, not find a new girlfriend.

She expressed her satisfaction that Lola had agreed to speak to me, and asked me what was written on the piece of paper her daughter had given me.

'Trade secrets,' I joked awkwardly.

'Well, at least she's talking to you. You're lucky. She never says anything to me at all any more. It's horrible. When kids are little, they spend hours telling you about every little scratch on their knee, and then as they get older they hide their darkest sorrows from you.'

'That's true.'

'It's ridiculous,' she said, suddenly looking sad. 'Because I know a lot more about dark sorrows than I do about little scratches.'

But her sadness was quickly forgotten when another character suddenly appeared (this scene was beginning to read like a soap opera script): Patrick returned home from work. He seemed astonished at the way his wife was dressed. At last he smiled coldly and said: 'I suppose I can't compete with literature.' I was saddened by his coldness, after our lunch had been so amiable. Whenever I was with one of my characters, I felt as if I lost some of the complicity I'd established with the others; it was like an emotional seesaw. I could understand his reaction, though: his wife was going out to dinner with another man, and she was making no attempt to disguise her desire to be attractive. Unwittingly, I had ended up in the middle of their marital crisis. I wanted some exciting incidents for my book, of course, but I didn't want to end up writing a bedroom farce. Patrick's reaction made me think about cancelling our dinner date; but if I did that, I risked losing it all, risked destroying everything I'd achieved up to then.

I said something friendly in response, but he disappeared into his room without a word. I knew I hadn't done anything wrong, so I put his attitude down to his stressful work situation. He was obviously on edge. As for Valérie, she seemed surprised: 'It's strange seeing him react like that. Usually he doesn't give a damn what I do. I had the feeling I could go out for dinner with Brad Pitt and he wouldn't even bat an eyelid. Apparently I was wrong

…' I wanted to tell her what I knew: that her husband might have been incapable of expressing this recently, but he loved her. But that wasn't what she saw at all. Once she'd got over the initial shock, all she perceived in her husband's behaviour was misplaced bitterness. She was deeply unimpressed by his attitude. It was intolerable, she said, to bemoan a situation while doing nothing to fix it. I even heard her hiss: 'It's pathetic.' Relations between the two of them were more explosive than ever.

47

We took our seats in a charming little bistro. Valérie explained that she'd never been here before: 'I often walk past it though. I've always dreamed of coming in, but I was waiting for the right occasion.' She wanted us to order drinks straight away. 'Why don't we get some champagne to start?' I wasn't sure what I could do to curb her enthusiasm. Of course I was thrilled that she was so invested in the evening; this was an opportunity for me to get to know my character even better (I wanted to know more, for instance, about the reasons behind the obvious tensions with her sister). But I was absolutely determined to avoid any ambiguities. While I liked this woman, I saw her above all with the eye of an entomologist dissecting a beetle. Clearly we were not on the same wavelength at that moment. Valérie's opening salvo confirmed my suspicions.

'Well, it's not every day that I go out for dinner with a writer. I mean, it is quite exciting.'

'I don't know why you think that. Writers are mostly pretty dull.'

'You're not. I think you're quite sparkling in your interviews. I've watched everything I can find on the internet. People adore you.'

'Not everybody.'

'Are you talking about *Le Masque et la Plume*? I listened to that show. It's true they were hard on you. But they're like that with everyone. Every time I listen to it, it's brutal. I think it's over the top, personally. You can critique a book without being so hateful. Frankly, all I feel for them is contempt.'

'Oh, don't say that. Your words might end up in my book, and I don't want them to take offence. I'm terrified of them. Say something nice about them, please!'

'Seriously?'

'Yes.'

'Um, all right … I think it takes a lot of courage … to express your opinion so strongly … Is that okay?'

'Yes, very good. Keep going.'

'Well, it's true that everything's a bit half-hearted these days. It's good to hear some passion. And they're often right. Their opinion means a lot to me. We're lucky to have such excellent cultural guides.'

'Perfect! And maybe you should say they're attractive too …'

'Now you mention it, that's true … they have beautiful voices. It's like honey in my ears.'

'…'

I shot Valérie the relieved smile of someone who's just been acquitted of a crime.

48

The waiter wandered nonchalantly over to our table, then began speaking very fast.[14] Consequently, I didn't really hear what he said about the dish he most recommended, but I ordered it anyway. Valérie took her time looking at the menu. She kept hesitating, changing her mind, and the waiter grew annoyed. He kept smiling though. Another dichotomy: pleasant irritation. In the end, she opted for the same dish as me, adding coquettishly: 'I can't help being influenced by you!' This woman missed no opportunity to flirt. And the more I drew for her an unflattering picture of myself, the more she seemed to admire my self-deprecation. It is very difficult to change someone's opinion about you, whether positive or negative, once they've made up their mind. I could always become insufferable, but if I did that I risked losing her. Apart from a few masochists, very few people are likely to want to confide in a psychopath. So what was I to do? My position was starting to appear untenable.

Valérie continued her inquisition. No matter how much I protested that I didn't want to talk about myself, she kept interrogating me. Anyone would have thought she wanted to write a book about *my* life. She sipped her champagne, then her wine, and asked me increasingly intimate questions. This really wasn't going well. I couldn't stop the flood of seductive looks and hints. I felt as if I was Marty McFly in *Back to the Future*, meeting

14. I had never seen such rhythmic discordance between walking and talking before.

his mother during his journey into the past. In the film, the hero's young mother falls for him in a big way, endangering his future existence: if she doesn't fall in love with his father, little Marty will never be conceived. The same was true for me now: I was altering the trajectories of the lives I wanted to describe.

I had agreed to answer one question about myself per day, but this was getting out of hand. She wanted me to talk about Marie. How we met, what we were like together, how it ended. It was all so complicated: how can you summarise the life and death of a love affair? I can admit it now, and Valérie will only learn this by reading these lines, but I decided I had to lie to her.

'After my last conversation with you, that very evening, I wrote to Marie. I asked her if she still preferred solitude to me. She replied straight away, and we've exchanged a few messages. I think both of us are happy that we're back in touch. I've learned a lot from her recently. I wasn't supportive enough when she needed me. And that made her want to step away from the relationship. But, reading her messages, I get the feeling that she misses me a little bit. So we decided to see each other again. In fact, all of this is kind of thanks to you. It was your reaction that prompted me to write to her.'

'That's wonderful,' Valérie exclaimed, with an enthusiasm that took me by surprise.

'Yes, it is wonderful,' I replied, thinking: if only it were true.

Inevitably I started thinking about Marie again. I hadn't sent her a message. She'd left my life slowly and gently, without any fuss, as if silently erasing herself. I knew it had all been my fault; I hadn't been there for her. Several times she'd tried talking to me about it, but I hadn't listened. Why had I retreated into my shell like that? I regretted it bitterly now, but it was too late. I have so often lived my life belatedly. I'm the kind of person who comes up with a brilliant retort only when the person who insulted me is already far away. I could try to explain everything to Marie now. Tell her I'd been going through a strange phase when life seemed to lose its flavour and I'd had no appetite for anything. A sort of depression that had blinded me to our happiness. There are times in life when you blithely trample over wonders. Actually I just told you that I'd had no appetite for anything, but that isn't true. I'd had an appetite for destruction. Thinking back, I had the feeling that I didn't deserve Marie. Didn't deserve the love we shared. I knew where to look for the source of such fears. Deep down, I knew all of that. But I didn't want to admit it to myself. I was tired of talking about me. So I let myself drift back inside my shell.

'Aren't you listening to me?' Valérie asked.

'Of course I am.'

'What was I talking about?'

'You ... All right, it's true, I was miles away just then.'

'It's okay. But you're not like me: when I'm thinking about something else, nobody can tell! I always imagine that the other person will look in my eyes and realise I'm not paying attention. But it never happens. I just return to the conversation as if nothing happened. But you're so transparent: it was obvious your mind was elsewhere.'

'You'll have to give me your secret. I'm terrible at hiding things.'

'I just hope you're not bored ...'

'No, not at all. You got me talking about myself, and that set me thinking. Anyway, I'm sorry. You were saying?'

'Nothing special. Just that I was happy for you. And I was telling you about a couple I know who got back together after a separation.'

'Oh yeah, I get the impression that's happening more and more these days.'

'Is it? I don't know. But anyway, I think they realised that they were even more miserable apart from each other than they had been together.'

'Well, that's one reason to get back with someone,' I said, without believing it.

After this digression, Valérie returned to her favourite subject: me. During our first conversation, she'd thought I was trying to play down the pain I'd felt at losing Marie. So she was really happy to learn that things were looking up. Her reaction made me feel stupid. I had been totally wrong about her intentions.[15] Her enthusiasm did not seem faked in the slightest. She spoke to me with even more friendliness and warmth than before. Evidently I wasn't seeing things clearly. She might be disappointed by her marriage, but that didn't mean she was imagining herself with another man. She would mention this herself in a few minutes, in fact.

I had been wrong to stick too firmly to my principles. What was preventing me writing about Valérie after a conversation about both of our lives? I started to enjoy our discussion, and the thoughts it was provoking. By interrogating me about Marie, she had forced me to put what I'd experienced into words. Something I'd never done before, or not enough anyway. Whenever some of my friends tried to get me to talk about it, I would always change the subject. Whereas now I found myself amazed by the slightly autobiographical turn that this book was taking. But that's always how it is: only by moving away from things are you able to get closer to them. Rushing into the lives of others, I had ended up meeting myself. But was that something I wanted to do?

---

15. It is perhaps in my relationships with women that I am most obviously a writer of fiction.

49

Valérie felt more or less the same way. She ended up talking about herself, telling me that our meeting had acted like a catalyst. 'I've realised so many things since you started asking me about myself. Everybody should have someone like you in their life: a writer lacking inspiration.'

'That's kind of you.'

'I'm joking, but it's true. In the past two days, I've seen everything in a different light.'

'For example?'

'I feel like I can't wait any more. My light is going out. I didn't have to talk to you for long before realising that everything was wrong with my life. I'm forty-five, and I feel a sort of urgent need inside me. It can't go on like this.'

'It's normal to go through periods of doubt.'

'This isn't doubt, it's a fact.'

'So you really want to leave your husband?'

'Yes.'

'I'm not going to judge you, but I have the impression that you're being a bit hasty. That things aren't as black and white as you seem to believe.'

'Maybe, but I need to make a decision. I need to move forward. To change my life.'

'You could do things gradually.'

'What does that mean? Take a lover? I don't want that.'

'No, I meant taking some time for yourself …'

'Like going on holiday alone for a week? Do you seriously think that's what I need? I'm not interested in half-measures. I need to make a decision and be clear.'

'…'

'Don't make that face. I'm ready to deal with the consequences. I'm even ready to be proved wrong. But my life can't go on like this.'

A silence fell then, mainly because I didn't know what to say. She seemed determined to leave her husband, but there had been no hint of tragedy in her voice. I continued to believe that she wasn't fully aware of the significance of her words. Sometimes people announce a big decision in a fit of passion. But once that decision is made, they're confronted with a radical new reality. She didn't seem, to me, to be taking into account the suffering her choice would create. She hadn't mentioned Patrick's probable devastation or how her children would feel. There comes a moment in many people's lives where they see only their own survival, and I could completely understand that. She'd talked about an urgent need, then she'd said, almost with a smile: 'Life's too short.' The phrase everyone uses when their lack of fulfilment becomes unbearable.

50

Not only did Valérie seem to lack clarity about the emotional drama she was about to unleash on her family, but she was growing increasingly cheerful. Admittedly, we were close to finishing our second bottle of red. I had to slow down or I would no longer be capable of transcribing what we said to each other. But I was surrendering to the pleasure of the evening, sometimes completely forgetting I was there to work. Then again, that is pretty much the definition of a writer: we never really know when we're working. It's the kind of profession that allows you to sit there doing nothing for hours on end while claiming that you're in the middle of a huge undertaking.

Between all the alcohol and the released emotions, I had forgotten to tell Valérie about the trip I would soon be making with her mother. When I did finally announce this, she burst out in hysterical laughter. The vision of me travelling to the other side of the world with Madeleine seemed utterly ridiculous to her. 'I think you're losing the plot!' she told me, pouring us some more wine. Easily influenced, I found myself wondering if she was right. I had imagined our trip as a fascinating, romantic adventure, but what if it was merely risible? What was I going to do in Los Angeles with an elderly person I barely knew? But I decided to put my doubts to one side. I was strapped into the rollercoaster of my mind again. As before, I had feared Valérie's reaction to my news – baselessly, as it turned out. I'd even thought she might try to stop us leaving. That was why I'd bought the flight tickets without telling her, so I could present her with a fait accompli. But in fact, she told me that she thought it was a wonderfully batty thing for her mother to do. In a softer voice, she added: 'All of this is like a balm for her heart, you know.'

I thought this phrase was not only true but beautiful. Probably wrongly, I also saw it as an allusion to the conflict between Valérie and her sister, which must have caused Madeleine some heartache. So our trip would do her good; it would *take her mind off things*, as the saying goes. If only one's mind could really be 'taken off' things as easily as taking a wine glass off a table. I saw an opening and tried once again to get Valérie to talk about this painful subject.

'Ah, my sister ... Do you really want to ruin our evening?'

'Not at all.'

'I do miss her, you know,' she said suddenly, with a hint of sadness in her voice. But it was a sadness inspired by alcohol. Drunkenness is like a fork in the road that can lead in two very different directions: towards hawkishness or mawkishness, towards bitterness or forgiveness. Apparently Valérie had taken the second path.

'You should call her and tell her that.'

'I can't. We stopped talking a long time ago. I can't even remember when our last conversation was.'

'Is that why she went to Boston?'

'Probably. It was all very sudden.'

'...'

TWO SISTERS

Valérie was born just over a year after Stéphanie. Quite soon, though, it became almost impossible to tell which was the elder of the two. They shared everything, the same hobbies and the same friends, to the point where they were often described as inseparable. They went to see Michael Jackson in June 1988 at the Parc des Princes, and The Cure at the National Music Festival in Place de la République in 1990. One girl's memories bled into the other's; sometimes they weren't sure who had done what, so closely connected were their lives. This was the first movement of an idyllic relationship.

It was hard to pinpoint exactly when things began to change. The poison of rivalry gradually seeped between the two siblings. Maybe it was caused by a boy who preferred one of them to the other. Could a look from some Theo or Leo really have destroyed such an intensely close sisterhood? No, it was absurd. What then? Well, there was the skiing accident. But it seemed crazy to imagine that all their tensions could have stemmed from that. Even so, it was a theory that Valérie no longer dismissed. Without doubt, there had been a *before* and an *after* that fall.

The two sisters had been having fun together on the slopes during the February school holidays. They weren't sleeping much, since they would keep talking with their friends in the dorm long after the lights went out. So fatigue probably played a role in what happened. In the afternoons, they were allowed to go skiing without the rest of the group. After all, they were fifteen or sixteen. They loved stopping at the top of the mountain and lying on deckchairs outside the piste-side bar. Both girls were very sporty, but they also enjoyed doing nothing sometimes, basking in the sun that seemed so close up there. Behind their sunglasses, they watched the older boys, both of them hoping they wouldn't be considered too young. Those moments were as close to pure happiness as they'd ever felt.

It was during one of those glorious days, as they skied back down to the resort, that they both took a heavy fall. Without even thinking about it, they'd decided to descend the slope while listening to a Walkman, sharing the same pair of earphones. Valérie had forgotten to bring hers. They loved listening to music while they skied, and they wanted to descend to the sound of the Pixies song, 'Where Is My Mind?'. Obviously it was dangerous, but they were excellent skiers, and the piste that led down to the resort was a relatively easy blue run. They enjoyed skiing like that, with their skis close together and their heads leaning in to share the same song. But all it had taken was a small bump and one of them had been jolted sideways, their skis had crossed, their legs had tangled, and they'd both been taken down in a violent fall. Stéphanie began howling with pain, while Valérie was unscathed. The emergency services arrived pretty quickly and the injured girl was taken down to the resort on a sledge. An ambulance transported her to the hospital in Chambéry. The X-rays revealed a double fracture of her tibia. For two hours, Stéphanie brooded anxiously on a trolley in a hospital corridor, with no news of her sister. This was before the era of mobile phones. Valérie, meanwhile, was at the resort, trying to find out what had happened to her sister, and when she was told that Stéphanie was at the hospital she caught a bus there. Together again, they hugged. Her sister's injuries weren't really so bad, Valérie thought; she seemed more shaken than anything. But of course it meant the end of Stéphanie's holiday. The next day, she would travel back to Paris, accompanied by Madeleine, who had left work in the middle of the day and caught the next flight to see her daughter.

Valérie stayed for the second week of the holiday and

made some new friends. It was sad, but it wasn't a big deal. The two sisters talked on the phone and Stéphanie told her: 'Have fun for me.' All the same, she couldn't help wondering: 'Why me and not her?' There was no anger in this thought, it was simply an observation that a single act had led to two radically different outcomes. Bedridden and bored, she kept brooding on the situation, while Valérie continued hurtling down ski slopes. Fate had favoured her sister. The same question kept repeating on a loop – 'Why me and not her?' – like an annoying tune she couldn't get out of her head.

Something else needs to be mentioned here. Taking advantage of the fact she was alone, Valérie grew closer to Malik, the young ski instructor on whom both sisters had a crush. At the last-night party, Malik couldn't help noticing the way Valérie kept staring adoringly at him. After a few drinks, he ended up kissing her in a dark corner, before remembering how young she was and realising this was not a good idea. He made his excuses and left then, but the kiss – however brief – had really happened. Naturally, Valérie told her sister all about it, unaware of how deeply the information would affect her. For Stéphanie, it felt like salt rubbed in her wounds. For an instant she even wondered if Valérie had planned the whole thing. Had she caused the accident to get rid of Stéphanie, leaving the coast clear for her to get what she wanted? Perhaps the painkillers she was taking were fogging her brain, but in any case it was probably at that moment that she started to resent her sister.

While the two of them appeared outwardly as close as ever, Stéphanie had begun to mistrust Valérie. She no longer shared all the secrets of her private life with her sister, and now and then she would arrange to go out without telling her. Valérie was surprised by this, but it wasn't so strange after all; they weren't obliged to do everything together. The following year, when the ski season came round again, Stéphanie decided to go to the mountains with one of her friends instead. It was the first time they'd gone skiing separately. Valérie could not understand this decision. Particularly since it would have been easy enough to invite Valérie to go with them. But it was what it was. She must still be traumatised by the accident, Valérie thought, and the idea of skiing together would just bring back painful memories. But Stéphanie didn't talk about any of that; she was just happy to be invited to join the family of one of her friends. She smiled as she ended their sibling ritual.

And so it went on. More and more frequently, Stéphanie would plan to do things without her sister. Cinema visits, shopping trips, parties. Valérie couldn't help but think: 'It's not like it was before.' This made her sad, but she didn't dare mention it. Why should she make the first move when her sister didn't want to be with her? She had no idea that the annoying tune was still stuck in Stéphanie's head: 'Why me and not her? Why me and not her?' And things didn't get any better. After the Malik episode, there was another boy problem. For a few weeks, Valérie had been going out with Benoît, a slightly older boy who played in a rock band. It was a cliché, of course, a seventeen-year-old girl hung up on a guitar hero. But that didn't make it hurt any less when he didn't call her for a week. She was deep in the throes of first love. She sought comfort from her sister, but Stéphanie seemed incapable of uttering a single word. Her look said: 'You've got a cool boyfriend and I'm alone. Do you really expect me to console you when he goes off somewhere?' There could be no doubt about it now: Valérie's sister was jealous. It was the kind of jealousy that murders all kind feelings. For Stéphanie, the episode with Benoît had been just like that fateful ski trip. They'd met him together at a rock concert, but he'd preferred Valérie. Whenever they were side by side, she was always the one who stumbled.

In her paranoia, Stéphanie would sometimes think: my sister is a shadow cast over my future, a thief of possibilities. She is the one preventing me from living the life I want to live.

So often, children from the same family are compared. Which is absurd: just because you have the same upbringing does not mean you will have the same abilities or the same aspirations. Naturally, a child's early years are crucial for their development, but their own choices play an even greater part: how many chaotic lives have come from cosseted childhoods? How many brilliant achievements have arisen out of abusive infancies? Stéphanie knew all this; she shouldn't have let herself get caught in this futile competition. Especially since she kept losing. After the ski episode and the rock star episode came the most important of all: exams. It was the most important because, unfortunately, exams are how our society measures a person's capacities, at least during the early stages of life.

After passing her *baccalauréat*, Stéphanie had failed the entrance exam for Sciences-Po. There was nothing too tragic about this, except that, the following year, Valérie's application was accepted. Everyone in the family was thrilled and they opened a bottle of champagne to celebrate, even though nothing had been settled at that point: she still hadn't taken her oral exam. For Stéphanie, this glorification of Valérie's achievement just underlined her own failure. She continued down the road of this endless comparison. It was all the more ludicrous since the grades she was getting in her History degree were excellent. But her ego had been wounded and she seemed powerless to stop the spread of the narcissistic gangrene with each new insult to her pride. It is difficult to measure the amount of bitterness inside any soul.

There came a day, however, when her bitterness grew out of all proportion. Valérie was awaiting a letter announcing the date of her oral exam, but nothing came. This was before the internet existed, when it wasn't always easy to obtain information. In the end, she went to the university's administration office and was told that the orals had already taken place. She collapsed in sobs right there in the office, but it made no difference: she would not be able to join Sciences-Po that year. She had missed the second part of the exam, and that had ruined her chances. 'I didn't receive the letter!' she protested to the secretary who, seeing her so upset, felt sorry for her. The secretary explained that all the letters had been sent by registered post with a signature required on delivery. She checked in a file that Valérie's letter had not been returned, which proved that someone had received it on her behalf. Valérie thought instantly of her sister. So, somewhere deep inside, she had sensed the insidious vibrations of Stéphanie's jealousy. She couldn't simply accuse her, however. Stéphanie would deny it, she would act offended, she would make herself the victim: how could her own sister possibly believe her capable of such an act? Besides, there was no way of proving her guilt.

The family asked their neighbours and the building's concierge if any of them had signed for the letter, but their investigation hit a dead end. There was no trace of the letter anywhere. In the end, Stéphanie said to her sister: 'I can see that you think it was me. You can't imagine how hurtful that is.'

And Valérie found herself obliged to reassure her: 'No, of course not, I know you would never do anything like that!' But her doubts remained.

They both ended up at the Sorbonne. Because Valérie refused to apply to Sciences-Po again, despite her parents' encouragement. The wound had been too deep, and she couldn't face waiting a whole year to get on with her life. And, in fact, she was happy at the Sorbonne. She'd just turned eighteen and she loved her new life, with its oceans of free time. At least the first few months had gone quite well, Valérie told me. She became close to her sister again, and it was almost the way it had been during their adolescence. Stéphanie passed on the previous year's class notes and helped her. It was handy, having a big sister who'd already cleared the way for her. But one day, there was a photocopy missing in the folder Stéphanie gave her, and Valérie's life was changed forever.

She couldn't stop thinking about that missing page. It was like a blank page in a story: an absence that makes it impossible to fully understand the succession of events. She went to her sister's bedroom in search of that page. Stéphanie's room was so neat and tidy; she was a methodical person, with a tendency to keep everything. Was that why she'd kept the proof of her crime? It made no sense. Unless, perhaps, she subconsciously wanted to be found out? A way of confessing her sins. In any case, when she discovered the delivery receipt for her invitation to the Sciences-Po oral exam at the bottom of a drawer, Valérie fainted. She lay there on the floor for a long time, unconscious. When she came to, she went to the bathroom and took a long shower; she needed to wash away what she'd learned.

She wished she could hide her discovery to avoid the

consequences, but that proved impossible. Her face told the story. Her mother asked her what was wrong, and Valérie had no choice but to reveal the truth. That evening, there was a long discussion between the two sisters and their parents. White-faced, Stéphanie tried to justify what she'd done. It was an impulse, she said, beyond her control. Valérie pointed out that the months of lying afterwards could hardly be explained as an impulse; indeed, they were proof of a remarkably cool head. Stéphanie begged for her sister's forgiveness; and Valérie would probably reach that point one day, but nothing could alter the seriousness of what had happened. Something between them had been broken. For now, Valérie refused to speak to her sister, and Stéphanie left France a few months later.

They had seen each other only once since then: at their father's funeral.

Valérie admitted to me that she hardly ever talked about this subject. Back then, many of their mutual friends had tried to reconcile them, in vain. Everyone had attempted to understand what Stéphanie had done, even finding excuses for it. But it was all over. Her mother kept her updated on Stéphanie's life, but Valérie felt nothing as she listened to news of her sister. That was perhaps the most awful sensation, in fact: that numbness. She felt no bitterness or anger; nothing more than a vague nostalgia for the time when they had still been close. Stéphanie had tried on several occasions to make peace; she'd sent gifts for Lola's birth, and then for Jérémie's, but Valérie had not replied; she couldn't say 'thank you' to her sister.

To lighten the atmosphere, I suggested that she and I go on a trip to Boston. First the mother, then the daughter: I could specialise in journeys of healing for the Martin family. Valérie repeated that the whole thing was behind her, that the wound had already healed, but I sensed that the pain continued to nag at her. Valérie had forgiven her sister, but she didn't want to see her again. Who knew, maybe one day things would change and they would be reunited? (She had admitted that she missed her sister, after all, albeit under the influence of alcohol.) That, of course, was Madeleine's dearest wish. And I felt sure that Valérie would offer that gift to her mother, before it was too late.

It was almost midnight already; time flies when you're sharing secrets. Even if I was there for my book, I had genuinely enjoyed her company that evening. I liked the way she talked about past hurts without complaining, the way she found the right balance between being truthful to her emotions and maintaining enough perspective to tell the story. She was a natural memoirist. 'Well, I've never been to a shrink in my life, so it's really a new feeling, talking about myself like this,' she said, before adding that she was starting to like it. She was terrified of becoming addicted to talking to me. What would she do once the book had been written and I'd abandoned her for other characters?

'We could still keep seeing each other,' I replied. 'I'd be very happy to do that, actually. It's true that, when I finish writing a novel, I normally leave my characters behind. But this is different ...'

She smiled. As I was saying those words, I had a fleeting thought for all my old characters. With the book finished, we had gone our separate ways. Was there life after The End? I have sometimes wondered if Markus is still with Nathalie, fifteen years after I brought them together in my novel *Delicacy*, and if they're happy, far away from my words.

It was time to leave the restaurant. I hadn't noticed that we were the last customers. The extras in this scene had discreetly left the set. The waiter looked relieved when we stood up to go, because it saved him an awkward conversation. He said 'goodbye' with exactly the same intonation as he'd said 'hello'.

Outside, the cool air felt like a blessing. A much-needed airing of our neurons. I don't know why I had let myself drink so much when I was already so tired and I needed to concentrate. Probably to keep up with Valérie. It's hard to have a nice evening with someone without a good liquid equilibrium. Two sober people have plenty to say to each other; two drunk people even more so; but would one sober person and one drunk person really be able to have a conversation? This theory was my justification for the way we were swaying as we walked. Valérie held my arm to stay on her feet, but she was clear-headed enough to guide us home. She repeated several times that she hadn't had so much to drink in a long time, and that it had done her good. And it's true, we were both in a happy mood. Two drunken strangers, together in the night, wandering slowly to prolong this moment of escape. I like periods of time disconnected from the rest of my life; those little instants insulated from everyday reality.

Strangely, whenever I have tried to express this feeling, things have gone awry. Out of superstition, I make it my habit never to say how happy I am.

Given the state she was in, I thought it a good idea to accompany Valérie to her door. Absorbed in our conversation, she hadn't even glanced at her phone all evening. So she hadn't seen all the (increasingly anxious) messages from her husband. Patrick was waiting for her in the living room, looking furious. He bore no resemblance to the man I'd had lunch with earlier that day. He charged at me, yelling: 'You've come here to destroy our family!'

'What?' I gasped. 'No ... that's not—'

'I should have known better. Why the hell did I agree to any of this? Go on, piss off home!'

'You can't talk to him like that! Calm down!' Valérie said, belatedly losing her temper, as if it had taken her a few seconds to register her husband's hysteria.

'Don't you start! What the hell do you think you're doing, coming home drunk with a man at one in the morning!'

'I just walked her home,' I said.

'Shut your mouth! Go home and leave us in peace. You can write your stupid fucking book without us!'

'Stop it!' Valérie yelled.

'You keep out of it. This is between us. Go to bed!' Patrick said, grabbing his wife's arm.

'Don't touch me!'

Just then, the two of them turned to discover Jérémie and Lola standing in the hallway, faces frozen in shock and fear.

Valérie went over to them.

'Go back to bed, it's all right.'

'But you're yelling, Maman. What's going on?'

'Nothing. Your father's going crazy!'

'Oh, *I'm* going crazy? Jesus, I've heard everything now! As you can see, your mother's the one who's losing it. She's drunk. Anyway, go back to bed like we told you!'

'Are you sure it's okay?' Lola asked, glancing anxiously at her father.

'Yes, of course!' said Patrick, trying to speak more calmly this time.

The two teenagers didn't budge. In the end, Valérie walked them back to their bedrooms, speaking to them in a quiet, reassuring voice. So I found myself alone with Patrick, who glared at me. I had a simple choice: leave or get punched in the face. I decided to take the first option.

53

So I left the Martins' apartment without even saying goodbye to Valérie. I stood on the dark landing outside the door for a while, just to make sure that the situation was under control. Oddly, I wasn't worried. Patrick had flown off the handle, but I didn't really believe he was violent. Eventually I heard Valérie say: 'Don't say a word!', presumably as she came back into the living room, and then there was silence. Things seemed to have calmed down; I imagined them each retreating to a corner. I had the feeling that I'd been the trigger for what might be their final row; the kind of row you can't get over. I imagined Valérie brooding. What should I do? Send her a message? Or send one to Patrick? Apologising for what he must have thought, trying to calm the situation. I felt lost. Finally I decided it was better to let the storm pass. Or was it a hurricane? I wasn't sure what level of climatic metaphor to plump for.

Outside, I found a bench and sat down to gather my thoughts. Again, I was struck by the idea that their marriage would not survive the events of tonight. Valérie would never forgive him. She was possibly even ashamed of him, the fact that he'd behaved that way in front of me. She'd already been thinking of leaving him, but now he'd shot himself in the foot. In fact, those two things were almost certainly connected. Once you feel the person you love distancing themselves from you, it's not unusual to act in a way that further alienates them. Panic can bring out the uglier aspects of your personality. Love is often an act of self-sabotage.

Patrick had lost all perspective. His love for his wife had turned him into someone else. He could have greeted her with a smile, asking if she'd had a nice evening. Instead he acted like what he was: a wounded animal. Even so, I felt no urge to defend him. He was a drowning man, and he was trying to pull my project down with him. And, from my egotistical writer's point of view, that was the true disaster of the evening. He'd been perfectly clear: I wasn't welcome in his home any more. I found it hard to imagine him telling me anything else about his office ordeals. And he would stop the other family members from talking to me. Which meant that, after 37,779 words, I had now reached a dead end. There was only one thing left to write:

THE END

I sat there on the bench for a while. The night seemed to have hit the pause button too. Nobody walked past, and there were very few cars. Paris herself seemed short of inspiration. At last I stood up and started to walk home. After a few yards, I felt hope stir within me. Walking is always a source of comfort. I could invent the rest of the Martins' story. Yes, that was what I thought. If all else failed, I could always turn it into a novel.

As soon as I got home, I knew I wouldn't be able to sleep. I went to the bathroom and splashed some water on my face. But I wasn't trying to sober up. The scene at the Martins' apartment had already achieved that. Looking at myself in the mirror, I had to admit that I had never been very good at lighting. In the stark brightness of a strip light, my face had a sallow, pasty look. This was bad timing: already filled with doubt, I needed the reassurance of a more appealing reflection. The hope I'd felt on my walk back shrivelled and died: it now seemed ludicrous to think that I could invent an end to my characters' real lives. I had to choose a side: reality or fiction. I didn't believe that you could mix the two. Of course, I still had the trip with Madeleine. But would that be enough? And there was no guarantee that Yves Grimbert would turn out to be an interesting character. I felt a tide of pessimism rise over me. Nothing had the power to excite me now. I wanted to wallow in an orgy of Lagerfeld.

It was while in the depths of this literary despair, sitting on the cold tiled floor of the bathroom, that I picked up my phone and sent a message to Marie. It was almost 2 a.m., and I knew the impression my message would give: in the world of love, anything sent after midnight was almost certainly written in the grip of depression. It would be much better to wait until tomorrow afternoon and send her an inoffensive, falsely reassuring little text. At two in the morning, she was bound to think I was cracking up, that I was dying without her, and let's be honest: she wouldn't be completely wrong. But the conversation with Valérie had left me with an urge to find out how she was. Plus there was the context, of course: a highly eventful evening. When you feel fragile, you are bound to miss the person with whom you used to share everything. A problem shared is a problem halved, as they say.

And what was wrong with telling someone you missed them? Yes, that was all I had to say. Then maybe add: Thinking of you. Yes, Thinking of you. That's not too much. In fact, you could almost describe it as friendly.[16] I hoped she wouldn't think it was too pushy or pathetic. If she felt like that, I would rather she didn't reply. A simple, cold, distant 'thank you' would have been unbearable. Or worse, 'thank you very much', which would plunge us irreversibly into the world of bloodless politeness. Yes, it would be better not to get any reply at all. I sent that message the way earthlings emit signals into outer space, to check for extraterrestrial life. Yes, that's all my message was: a simple method of declaring that I was still alive.

Then something kind of crazy happened: she replied almost instantaneously. I checked several times that it was really her and not some sort of hallucination. I read the name slowly: M-A-R-I-E. She said it was so good to hear from me. For just a second, I wondered why she wasn't asleep at that time of night. Usually, she loved going to bed before midnight. Perhaps she wasn't alone? What an idiot I was, ruining a wonderful moment with such pointless thoughts. I needed to focus on the essential fact: she had replied to me *immediately*. She hadn't pretended. She hadn't done what most people do, waiting a while before replying to show that they are not desperate for human connection. Nothing is more beautiful than offering yourself to someone else straightforwardly with an immediate response.

16. Although friendship exists far less at night.

And her response was divinely simple too. She just wrote that she was happy to hear from me. And that she hoped I was well. We exchanged a few nice messages, concluding with our mutual desire to meet up again soon. And this wasn't a novel, it was reality: we had made plans to see each other. I couldn't get over the strange turn this evening had taken: from a painful confession to shared laughter; from a relationship that was dying to one being reborn.

56

I wanted to get off the rollercoaster, so I went back to my desk. I'd summoned enough energy to do my duty, to stick to the rule I'd set myself: noting down the latest news on my book every evening.

WHAT I KNOW ABOUT MY CHARACTERS (3)

Madeleine Tricot. Showed surprising boldness, coming to my apartment to see me. She asked me to go with her to Los Angeles. I exchanged a few messages with Yves Grimbert on Facebook, then booked our flights: I was taken aback by how simple this whole process seemed. Though I'm less optimistic about other aspects of the book, I remain very enthusiastic about witnessing this reunion. And finding out the reasons for Yves's departure.

Patrick Martin. Two contrasting tones in our conversations today. A pleasant, almost friendly lunch when he cooperated fully with my enquiries, telling me about his career and his current professional difficulties. Tomorrow (a few hours from the time I am writing this), he will be in a meeting with his new boss, Jean-Paul Desjoyaux. He fears he is going to be fired. After talking about work, Patrick and I moved on to the subject of his marriage. He thinks I can't understand. That is probably true. He concluded our interview with a declaration of love for Valérie. Unfortunately, the trust between us was shattered this evening when he saw me coming back late from dinner with his wife. Seeing her like that – tipsy, on my arm – sent him into a rage. Our brief friendship is clearly over, and he no longer wants me to write about his family.

Valérie Martin. I love this character! I really enjoyed her company at dinner. She asked me far more personal questions than I was comfortable with, but she also answered all my questions with unflinching honesty. Particularly regarding the long and painful story of her relationship with her sister. Thinking back, I find it really strange that Stéphanie kept the delivery receipt. I remember a similar story where the culprit acted in the same way. There is perhaps a feeling of omnipotence in certain crimes, driving the criminal not to destroy the proof of their misdeed. Chaotic/dramatic end to the evening with Patrick. Their marriage is going through a complicated, painful period. I don't know how things will end between them.

Jérémie Martin. Used me as a private tutor. Gave me a chance to reread François Villon, confirming my suspicion that medieval poetry is really not my thing. Give me Paul Éluard any day! Still not much to say about this character.

Lola Martin. Against all expectations, she confided in me about a very personal subject: her first time with a boy. This seems strange, but reflecting on it now, I think I understand what she's up to. Why would Lola trust me with such information when, up to that point, she had shown nothing but contempt for my project? Perhaps, by asking me to meet her boyfriend, she is bringing him into the cast of my book. Which will force him to act more responsibly. You can do things in life that you would never do if you knew they might be publicly revealed in a book. Lola realised she could use my status as a writer to serve her own interests. For the first time in my life, I am being manipulated by one of my characters.

57

Sometimes it feels as though you have lived through several days in the space of twenty-four hours. That was exactly how I felt as I went to bed that night – as if I'd woken up on Tuesday and was falling asleep on Friday.

The next morning, opening my eyes and turning on my phone, I saw I'd received a message from Valérie: EVERYTHING IS BACK TO NORMAL. SORRY FOR THE END TO OUR EVENING. RUNNING LATE — I'LL TELL YOU MORE AFTER WORK. I reread this message several times. That first sentence intrigued me. What did 'back to normal' mean? That Patrick had calmed down? That their marital problems had been solved? I couldn't find a path that would plausibly lead me through the labyrinth of those three enigmatic words. In any case, it struck me as good news for my book. If everything had calmed down, I would be able to go to their apartment again without being regarded as an intruder or an enemy. Then again, I had the impression that Valérie had written the message quickly, to reassure me. The situation might actually be more muddled than she wanted to admit. Or, worse, it was possible that she hadn't even written this message herself. Maybe Patrick had murdered his whole family and taken his wife's phone. This is a well-known tactic among murderers, as a way of buying time: they write texts, pretending to be their victims.

59

There is always a moment when you let yourself imagine the darkest possible version of a story. But let's be honest: the way things were at this point, it was hard to know whether my book was about to turn into a Stephen King novel or something by Barbara Cartland.

As I waited to find out what would happen next (particularly the outcome of Patrick's meeting wth Desjoyaux), I felt a bit lost. I could have spent the day writing down what I already knew, but it seemed to me that I ought to live through this story before I started telling it. I even thought it would be counterproductive to retreat into my shell now to transform acts into words. But what could I do today with the Martins? I had to let Madeleine prepare for our trip. In the end, I could think of only one course of action: meeting the famous Clément.

I sent him a message and he replied a few minutes later, in a break between two classes, I imagined. Lola must have told him about me because he immediately agreed to meet me that afternoon, in a café near their school. What was I going to say to him? I was supposed to find out if his intentions towards Lola were honourable. I was now beginning to understand what she was hoping to achieve. I was like an ambassador, there to ensure his legitimacy, to act as a sort of moral witness. But what could I actually do? Threaten him if he treated her badly? 'I'm warning you, son, if you dump her after sleeping with her, I'll write a very unflattering portrait of you in my book!' That was, I think, more or less what Lola was hoping I would tell this kid.

Now I feel bad for being facetious. I am giving you the impression that I took all this lightly, as if it were just one more task to be ticked off the list before I could devote myself to other more important ones. If I decide to keep this part in my book, it's because I am fascinated by the subject. I could have written a whole novel on what it means to have sex for the first time. It's an enduring obsession that becomes an unforgettable moment; and it's also one of the rare events in your life that cannot be rehearsed. In reality, it's probably not a big deal if you make a mistake, but anyone of even a vaguely romantic nature tends to put themselves under an enormous amount of pressure. Beneath her haughty, casual attitude, Lola was fragile and anxious; she knew both the pro of the situation (her desire for the boy) and the con (his reputation). She was well aware of the hand she held, and now it was a battle between her body and her mind. I had to try and help her solve this equation, despite the fact that I myself was the type of person to procrastinate for hours over romantic feelings and carnal acts; I felt like a vegetarian who'd been sent to sort out a dispute in an abattoir.[17]

---

17. Albert Cossery uses a similar metaphor in *A Splendid Conspiracy*: a head louse in the kingdom of the bald.

61

Abit later that day, I again thought about Valérie's 'everything is back to normal'. I was finding it ever harder to believe. It was the type of message you send hastily in the morning to reassure the witness of a disaster. I imagined that she wanted me to write it down in my book, to immediately alter the reader's opinion. I had to be careful: my characters were capable of falsifying reality to present themselves in the best possible light.

I didn't want to call Valérie, in case she thought I was being too pushy. I was there to follow them, not stalk them. I went round in circles, trying to work out what to do. To kill time, I packed my suitcase. It had been a while since I'd last travelled anywhere. Inevitably, I thought about Marie. Even the tag tied to the handle of my suitcase was a reminder of our last journey together. Tangible proof that we had known happiness. We had gone to Budapest; as if hiding behind that destination, all the other cities we'd visited together rose up to the surface of my mind. And so, as I chose what to pack for Los Angeles, I remembered Venice, Vienna, Reykjavik. I missed all our elsewheres terribly, and now I found myself wishing that it was the two of us going away together. Marie and I had only agreed to go out for a coffee, but I yearned for Istanbul to be hiding behind that cup.

When were we going to meet up? We had made no precise plans during our nocturnal chat, merely expressed a simple wish. Who should write to the other first? It all seemed so complicated now. I had been responsible for re-initiating contact between us, so wasn't it her turn to write to me now? Time had passed since our separation, and I'd got used to no longer hoping to see her name appear on my phone screen. But by getting back in touch with her, I had also refamiliarised myself with the purgatory of waiting for her messages.

62

Luckily, I didn't have the chance to wallow in such time-wasting reflections: I had to meet Clément. There's nothing quite like the lives of others to stop you living your own. I was glad I was waiting for him in a café rather than at the gates of the school. I didn't want to look like some paedophile predator. I often had the impression that people imagined the worst of me. (What? You think I'm paranoid? Does everyone think that?) I ordered a beer and soon afterwards saw a young man heading towards me. He must have Google-imaged me. Clément muttered that he was Clément and sat down facing me. I asked him what he wanted to drink. I sensed that he wanted a beer too, but he knew he had to make a good impression so he resisted the siren call of alcohol and asked for a Coke instead.

It was obvious that he felt uncomfortable with the situation. He might have found it funny or surprising, but his embarrassment was palpable. As if he had a guilty conscience. I was also surprised by his appearance: I'd expected a typical teenage hunk, the kind of guy who plays the guitar or goes surfing, the type who, when I was at school, would go out with all the girls while they chose me as their best friend. But he struck me as quite ordinary-looking, and not especially self-confident. For an instant, I even thought that Clément had sent one of his friends in his place. But no, it really was him. How could this young man be such a Casanova? How could Lola have fallen in love with him? I wanted to ask him about his methods. It could be a fascinating portrait: a teenage boy who doesn't look anything special but who possesses the secret of seduction.

After this moment of observation, mostly on my part, he started trying to find out a bit more about what was happening.

'So you're writing a book on Lola and her family?'

'Yes.'

'Why?' he asked, wide-eyed. 'Will people really read that?'

'I don't know. We'll see.'

'And I'll be in this book too?'

'Yes. Well, maybe.'

'I don't really get what I'm doing here. It's hard to understand. What exactly is your relationship with her?'

'There is none. I mean, I don't really know her. I'm writing a book, and she asked me to meet you.'

'Why?'

'To talk about your situation.'

'What is our situation?'

'You know it better than me, I guess.'

'Not really. I get the feeling she doesn't actually know what she wants. One day she wants to be with me, another day she just blanks me.'

'So what do you think is going on?'

'I dunno … she's a girl.'

'You don't think she's right to have doubts?'

'Why? We're good together. I don't see the problem.'

'She's worried you'll do to her what you did with the other girls. That's what she told me.'

'And what did I do?'

'You dumped them.'

'So? Is that a crime? I didn't love them.'

'I'm not judging you. I'm just telling you that the situation is making her uneasy. You must understand that …'

'It's weird talking to you about this. I don't know you. She's a big girl, isn't she? Can't she just tell me this herself?'

'Yes … of course …'

'So why's she sending you? Why's she getting you to say all this stuff?'

'It's not an easy thing for her to talk about. Maybe she thought, with someone on her side … things would be less … risky.'

'What risk are you talking about?'

'The risk of being disappointed, I suppose.'

'That's stupid. There's always a risk in life, don't you think?' he said, strangely mature all of a sudden.

'Yes, that's true.'

'Everything we're saying now, is it going to be in your book?'

'Maybe … I don't know.'

'Oh, I get it. You're going to turn me into a #MeToo bastard.'

'No, no …'

'Yeah, that's it. I don't trust you at all. This stuff is none of your business!'

'It was Lola who asked me to meet you.'

'Well, you should have said no! Haven't you got anything better to do than trying to solve some teenage girl's problems? You're a fucking pervert. Put that in your book! If you talk about me, write that I said that: you're an old perv!'

'…'

He stood up and hurried out of the café. I could have been disconcerted by the turn that our meeting had just taken, but my first thought was that this young man had an immense amount of charisma. Which explained everything. At only eighteen, he'd shown great self-assurance. I hadn't been able to control him. I was annoyed at myself for the way I'd handled the interview. But I could understand that he thought the whole situation was unfair and even stressful, given my position. Perhaps I could have told him that whatever he said to me would be 'off the record', as certain journalists do with politicians. But that wasn't my project; I was there to write down reality, even if the scenes fell flat or were cut short. In any case, at least he couldn't say I hadn't respected his wish to include his insult.

63

A few minutes later, I got a voice message from Lola. She was coldly furious. 'I hate you. Clément just dumped me. You're such an idiot. Last night my parents were yelling at each other and almost started hitting each other because of you. What are you trying to do with your stupid project – screw up our family? Well, congratulations, you did it. Bravo, Mr Writer! You're going to ruin everything. And I was stupid asking you to help me. So fucking stupid! It's obvious you don't understand anything about life. No wonder your wife left you.'

The venom in her message shocked me. I'd only done what she asked me to. Her intuition had led her to give me this bizarre mission, and now it had turned out a complete failure she blamed me for it. Surely she could have imagined that Clément wouldn't be happy to have to go through a sort of strange job interview. She knew him better than me, after all. In truth, not only did I understand his reaction, but I agreed with him on one essential point: love is innately risky. Lola was scared, and that was totally understandable. But all romantic relationships contain potential suffering. She could always sleep with a 'nicer' boy, but would she feel the same desire for someone like that? This reminded me of a line of dialogue in François Truffaut's *Mississippi Mermaid*, a scene that was reprised in *The Last Metro*:

GÉRARD DEPARDIEU
You're so beautiful that it hurts to look at you.

CATHERINE DENEUVE
You said it was a joy to look at me.

GÉRARD DEPARDIEU
It's a joy that hurts.

Lola wanted joy without pain, and I had tried to give her that. It was the first time she'd spoken to me and I'd hoped that my mission would lead her to start trusting me. Instead, another member of the Martin family now hated me. Perhaps this was how my book would end, with the five characters loathing and mistrusting the author. Like all those writers who use autobiographical elements in their stories and end up alienating everyone around them. I had to be careful before I was legally barred from publishing the book. Well, at worst, I could change the names. But I hoped that wouldn't be necessary. There had to be a middle ground between total reality and a lawsuit.

I went home, feeling slightly ashamed. I'd just been yelled at by a boy still young enough to be given homework. I had no desire to do anything; just then, writing struck me as the most stupid occupation possible for a human being. Or maybe the second most stupid, after fly-fishing, but I wasn't even sure about that. Lying on my bed, I thought about sending a message to Marie (despite my resolution to wait for her to write to me first), but even there I felt completely uninspired. You should be able to hire authors who could whisper the right lines to you at the right moment; textperts, digital Cyrano de Bergeracs. In reality, though, nobody could write the message for me, because I didn't even know what I wanted to say. Even at that low point, I wasn't desperate enough to send anything as redundant as THINKING OF YOU.

Thankfully, an event occurred to balance out the day's negative energies. Valérie called me to tell me what had happened the previous night. She began by asking me if she was disturbing me, calling so late. I glanced at the time on my phone screen: it was already almost midnight. How was that possible? I'd lost five or six hours in a temporal Bermuda Triangle. My mental ramblings had taken place in a world where hours lasted only minutes. I would often lose myself in the maze of my thoughts, but never before had so much time vanished without trace. In general, time flies when you're having a lot of fun. But for me, it was the opposite. Boredom fascinates me; it is in the depths of despair that I find myself misplacing whole hours.

'I'm sorry I didn't manage to call you earlier,' Valérie went on.

'That's all right. It's not a big deal.'

'Something amazing happened tonight.'

'Oh, really?'

'Yes, I can't believe it. And I think it might be thanks to you.'

'What happened?'

'It's Patrick ...'

'What?'

'I still can't believe it. It's ... it's ... I don't have the words ...'

'Tell me.'

'Well, I should probably start at the beginning, with what happened last night.'

'Yes, okay,' I said, trying not to show my impatience. I was so eager to find out about this mysterious event.

She began with the moment when I was standing on the dark landing outside their apartment door. The children had gone back to bed, and Valérie had taken a duvet from a cupboard and thrown it on the sofa. After twenty-five years of married life, this was the first time Patrick had been banished from the conjugal bed. It was a worrying sign. The 'separate rooms' stage often comes just before the 'separate lives' stage. In shock, he obeyed without a word. He knew he'd gone too far; he'd been incapable of controlling his aggression towards me. And yet, he wasn't generally someone who lost his temper. He wasn't the irascible type at all. In fact, you could even describe him as mild-mannered, quite reserved sometimes. His sudden rage that night, then, was completely out of character. Not that that made it any less intolerable in his wife's eyes. Valérie didn't want to talk to him any more. Not then, nor ever again. What had happened was the last straw for an already fragile relationship. How could he do such a thing? He'd shamed her, and shame is an emotion that does not fade easily. Even worse: he'd done it in the presence of a witness and their own children. When suffering turns to hysteria, that's one thing, but it has to remain private, invisible to others. So, yes, he had crossed more than one line.

She was brooding on all this in their double bed when she heard the door open. 'Go away. I told you I didn't want to talk to you. Leave me alone ...' But Patrick just stood there, wild-eyed in the doorway. He murmured something, too quiet to hear. As if he were speaking the secret language of silence. Valérie was furious at this half-hearted entrance; if you were going to burst into someone's room to beg for their forgiveness, you could at least speak up. And that was when she noticed something surprising: tears. Valérie stared at her husband's face. She couldn't remember ever seeing him like that before. Patrick hadn't cried since one of his friends died in a car accident in 1997. Although she couldn't explain why, this made a drastic difference to her state of mind. Yes, it was true: those few drops of salty water falling from her husband's eyes radically altered the situation, and maybe even her life.

He walked towards her, still crying. For the first time, he'd realised that he might lose the woman he loved; a mortal wound to his future happiness. The prospect of a night spent on the sofa was a premonition of the loneliness to come. And that destroyed him. So he let out what he'd been keeping locked inside for months. Everything he'd suffered at work came bursting out too. But the most important thing in his life was Valérie. He loved her, he knew he loved her, and he also knew how cruelly incapable he'd been of showing her that recently. It is often only when you are on the verge of losing someone or something that you truly understand how much they mean to you. His wife's voice and expression when she ordered him to sleep on the sofa had been like an electric shock for Patrick. He couldn't lose her. And the tears had come. Tears that kept pouring uncontrollably from his eyes.

Amid these tears, he tried to express his fear. His words were simple and disarmingly beautiful. 'I can't live without you. You're the love of my life. It was the fear of losing you that made me blow up like that. I'm so sorry, please forgive me …' She felt as if she'd rediscovered the man she used to love; yes, she was face to face with the sensitive side of her husband that had become, for her, a paradise lost.

She took his hand and he got into their bed.

They slept in each other's arms all night long.

Dreaming once again of the love they felt.

In the glorious daze of a marriage reborn.

At first, it struck me as strange that such vast bitterness and disenchantment could be swept away by a few tears. But it wasn't just the tears, it was also what Patrick had said: his declaration, like the last words of a man sentenced to death. Despite everything she'd told me, this was what Valérie had been waiting for: a reaction on her husband's part. They'd been brushing past each other for so long … Now, at last, she understood his distress, his pain. And it did them both good to talk and to cry (because she couldn't hold back the tears either). They realised that it had been years since they'd been so open with each other. Patrick wanted to send me a message, apologising, but Valérie told him she'd do it herself. Everything is back to normal.

That night of tenderness had left them both in a stupor. There is something sublime about discovering someone you've always known. Patrick got up to make breakfast. Everything he did radiated the promise of a new era. He went to wake his children, first Lola and then Jérémie, and apologised to them. He explained that his difficulties at work had darkened his moods. His children, now wide awake, were both understanding. He realised now that he didn't share his feelings enough with his loved ones. He'd let his doubts and fears seep into their home. It was stupid; you had to say what was on your mind, if only to garner some support. Both his children told him: 'It'll be okay, Papa.' And he wanted to cry again. His system was collapsing, and it was the best thing that could have happened to him.

He went to his office, filled with a new energy. When you rediscover the essence of your life, nothing else can scare you. He wondered why he'd let himself fall into such a spiral of anxiety. Of course he feared losing his job. But was it that important? He'd receive unemployment benefit, and he'd be able to enjoy life a little, to spend time with his family. And it was likely he'd be able to find another job, with his experience. While others had to endure harassment without any possibility of escape, he realised he would be in control of his own fate. His meeting would take place that day, and he was mentally preparing to be dismissed. Surely he would see it in Desjoyaux's eyes, the gleam of his perversity: the sadistic thrill of extinguishing a man's last hopes after three days of waiting. Because Patrick was under no illusions; he would soon be packing his belongings into cardboard boxes.

Late that morning, he received a message from Valérie: THINKING POSITIVE THOUGHTS FOR YOUR MEETING. Those words struck him as extraordinary. How long had it been since they'd written anything nice to each other? He scrolled through their recent texts and saw only CAN YOU BUY A BAGUETTE? or DON'T FORGET TO BRING A FOLDER FOR JÉRÉMIE. Messages in the form of orders. Commemorations of the ordinary. At what point does the lexicon of a love affair turn into something else? After two years, five years, ten? Texts become means of conveying practical information, a far cry from earlier expressions of love and romance.

He reread the message several times. He didn't want to reply simply: THANK YOU. In the end he wrote that her message was the strength he needed. It was borderline bombastic, maybe even a bit naff, but he wanted to express his true feelings now, whatever they were. A clumsy 'I love you' is always better than a sparkling but heartless one-liner. And Valérie was happy with this response, with these words that were bringing them back closer together. They were rediscovering each other.

68

He checked his phone: it was time for his meeting. At last he would confront his tormentor. But of course, this unbearable wait would not end as easily as that. A secretary explained that Desjoyaux was in the middle of a telephone meeting, and he would probably be a few minutes late. Patrick sat on a chair in the corridor, as if he were waiting for news in a hospital. To hide his anxiety, he began surfing the net on his phone; Twitter is the indoor equivalent of a cigarette. One of the celebrities he followed was Yoko Ono, who had just posted something mystical about peace and souls. He didn't fully understand it, but it seemed to suit his situation. Then again, what did she know about office life? He was a big Yoko fan, but it was easy to toss out mantras on the beauty of life and how every day was an opportunity waiting to be seized when you weren't about to have a meeting with Desjoyaux.

And that bastard continued to make him wait; his suffering wasn't over yet. After a while, Patrick wanted to get up and leave, an act that would probably have been tantamount to resigning. But he couldn't leave without knowing the truth; he wanted to find out why he'd been summoned. What had he done? Maybe a case that he'd mismanaged, although he couldn't think of one; objectively, his work was good. Nobody had ever had cause to complain about him, and all his clients remained faithful to him. So what could it be? A redundancy on economic grounds? He couldn't imagine anything else. They had to trim the workforce prior to another merger. But for the company, Patrick's salary was merely a drop in the ocean. Getting rid of him wouldn't change much, and would in fact cause problems with a number of cases. But Gerbier had had plenty of clients, and Desjoyaux had still fired him. They'd been redistributed to other employees' portfolios; accepting this overspill of work was simply expected. If anyone thought they were being worked too hard, well … they knew where the door was. There were thousands of keen young people out there, eager to replace them. The vast competition that existed beyond the walls of their headquarters, whether real or imagined, was relentlessly brought up.

The longer he waited, the more certain Patrick felt: he was no longer willing to make himself ill just to keep his job, no longer prepared to submit to one man's will. After an hour of waiting, he finally decided to leave – and, just then, the secretary told him Desjoyaux was ready to see him. He entered his boss's office with a calm, almost regal step. Desjoyaux told him to sit down without even looking at him, without even apologising for the one-hour wait. Everything was normal in the kingdom of contempt. Yet the strange thing was that if you didn't know him, you'd think Desjoyaux looked quite friendly. His body was tall and thin, but his head was perfectly round; a jovial face placed, as if by mistake, on an austere pedestal. Patrick knew the boss's orders: he was not to speak first. So he sat down in silence and waited for the man behind the desk to deign to raise his head. The comedy of power could begin.

Most discussion of bullying takes the viewpoint of the victims. But what is the psychology of the bully? What is he like at night, in darkness? Does he savour his power, without the faintest twinge of guilt? Desjoyaux would be a wonderful central character. I'd love to find out about his private life, his sexuality, his children (if he has any). Does he like to read? And, if so, is he more Proust or Céline? Camus or Sartre? This is another problem with reality;

I am not omniscient. When the book comes out, someone is bound to tell him that he's mentioned. Maybe he would like to balance out the caricature of him that I am sketching? I would like it if some of my characters could give their version of events afterwards.

'How are you, Martin?' he asked at last.

'Fine. Thank you.'

'Not too stressed?'

'No, I'm okay.'

'You can tell me anything. You know that, right?'

'Yes.'

'So you're really not too stressed?'

'Work is pretty intense at the moment, but I'm okay.'

'Well, seeing as you're not too stressed, can I give you some new clients?'

'...'

'No response?'

'I was thinking. You're the one who makes the decisions, of course, but in my opinion I already have enough on my plate. Especially since Lambert was fired.'

'You think we shouldn't have dismissed him?'

'He was good at his job.'

'Not as good as you.'

'...'

'And Martinez? What do you think of Martinez? You think he's a good employee?'

'Yes, of course.'

'So, as far as you're concerned, "everyone is good, everyone is nice" ... is that it?'

'No ... no,' said Patrick, increasingly embarrassed. 'But you're talking about my colleagues, and I know they work hard. That's all.'

'And if you were in my place and you had to fire someone, who would it be?'

'Sorry?'

'If you had to choose one person to fire, who would it be?'

'I can't answer that. I don't know ...'

'Come on, Martin. You're an intelligent man, you know the job, you understand this company better than anyone. So be frank: there's someone here who's underperforming. I have a little idea myself, but I'd love to know yours. For comparison purposes.'

'You're putting me in an uncomfortable position, if I may say so. I can't do that to a colleague.'

'Hmm ... well, I can't say I'm surprised. I can see why your career has stalled. You never take a risk. That's your choice, Martin. It's your choice. But I'm disappointed. I expect much more from you if you want to thrive in the new company structure.'

'You expect me to denounce my colleagues?'

'What? No, not at all! There's no need to jump to conclusions. "Denounce"! All I want is a frank exchange of views. I want your opinion. And that's also why I wanted to see you.'

'To get my opinion?'

'Yes. Haven't you noticed anything different about this office?'

'No,' said Patrick, after looking around.

'Are you sure?'

'Yes. I mean ... I don't know. I don't come to this office very often.'

'The curtains.'

'What about the curtains?'

'I had them changed.'

'Ah ...'

'I wanted to get your opinion.'

'On what? The curtains?'

'Yes, exactly.'

'You wanted my opinion … on your curtains?'

'How many times are you going to repeat that? I don't see what's so extraordinary about my request. I simply wanted your opinion on my new curtains.'

'That's why you wanted to see me?'

'Yes.'

'That's why you said it was *imperative* we meet? After a three-day wait?'

'Yes, because I wasn't entirely sure I'd made the right choice. So I thought: "I know, I'll ask Martin – I bet he's got a good eye for these things."'

'Me?'

'Yes. It was a hunch I had. Do you like this brown?'

'I don't know. Yes, they're good,' replied Patrick, staring numbly. The turn their conversation had taken had left him in a state of shock.

'They're good. Is that all you have to say?'

'…'

'Nothing about them bothers you? The diamond shapes aren't too much?'

'No.'

'All right. Well, I trust your judgement.'

'If that's why you … Can I … go now?'

'Yes, Martin, of course. You can. Always a pleasure to talk to you.'

'…'

Patrick exited Desjoyaux's office, leaving behind that strange conversation. The corridor he had to walk through to the lift seemed incredibly long. Each step took a huge effort. Finally, he stopped in front of the coffee machine, his mouth dry, but he couldn't decide what he wanted to drink.

A female colleague came up to him and asked: 'Are you okay? You're very pale.'

Not wanting to panic her, he replied that he was fine. But she decided she ought to stay with him for a while. Sophie – that was her name – suggested to Patrick that he go to her office and sit down for a few minutes. They walked there together, and he was free at last to relax, away from prying eyes. She brought him a glass of water, and a tissue so he could wipe the sweat from his forehead. He looked as if he was coming down with a fever.

Sitting in the office of this colleague whom he barely knew, he remembered what he'd heard about her. He wasn't sure if it was true or merely a rumour, but Patrick had been told several times that Sophie had seen her co-worker commit suicide. In the company where she used to work, she had shared her office with a man for a few years. One day, suddenly, while they were having a perfectly normal conversation about a film, he had stood up and jumped out of the window. Yes, Patrick recognised her now: she was the suicide girl. That's what they called her. He didn't know what conclusion to draw from this, but just as he'd been on the verge of fainting she'd been very kind and helpful to him. As he sat there drinking a third glass of water, she smiled at him.

Patrick's vision was oddly distorted. It took a while before it went back to normal, as if he were trying to refocus a complicated camera lens. He stood up and thanked Sophie for her help. He mumbled that he'd just felt suddenly tired – probably due to overwork. 'I need a holiday!' he'd declared, trying hard to sound light-hearted. Sophie hid her concern and told him simply that she was there if he needed anything. Presumably she was racked with guilt, constantly wondering what she could have done to save her colleague.

As he walked back to his office, Patrick gradually felt a weight lifting from his shoulders. The tension of the last few days dissolved. So he wasn't going to lose his job. But the interview confirmed his fears that the company was being run by a cynical monster. He wanted to laugh – he could have laughed – but his body had decided otherwise. It is always the body that decides these things. Deep down inside, in his flesh or in his heart, he was badly shaken. All those years he'd spent working there, being a team player, only to be humiliated. Because there was really no other word for what he'd just experienced: he'd suffered a crushing humiliation.

69

He sent a message to his wife, letting her know that everything was fine, then dealt with a few pressing work issues. He cancelled a meeting with a client, saying he was coming down with a fever. He didn't have the strength to travel across Paris to have a conversation about life insurance. Just for once, he thought, he could go to the cinema. Nobody was monitoring what he did with his time, and anyway he worked harder than anyone had a right to expect. So, yes, why not? Take the afternoon off and sit in a darkened room. See a film, it didn't matter which one. When was the last time he'd been to the cinema? He had no idea. Maybe some action movie he'd seen with his son. A *Mission: Impossible* or something like that. Yes, that was it. He remembered now: Tom Cruise on top of the tallest building in the world, in Dubai. Patrick was sitting in his office surrounded by Post-Its as he recalled that image of absolute heroism. He wondered fleetingly how Tom Cruise would have reacted to a meeting with Desjoyaux; how would his courage have manifested itself?

In the end, Patrick didn't go to the cinema that day; he went for a long walk instead. Something else he hadn't done for years. In fact, he'd forgotten what a weekday afternoon even looked like. He wandered around, ignoring the ringing of his phone. The business district was deserted at that time of day. All those men and women were busy in their offices, doing their very important jobs. He looked at the buildings surrounding him and imagined them as filing cabinets, their drawers full of humans. Suddenly everything struck him as ridiculous. He wandered into a gambling bar where he drank a beer and watched some horse racing. For an hour, he had the impression that he was feeling something close to happiness. In fact, he found himself trying to hold in what could be described as a sort of euphoria. He noticed the missed calls on his phone and thought about the days before mobile phones were invented, when you could genuinely disappear from your life.

70

At rush hour, as people in suits swarmed out of office buildings and down into the metro, Patrick was making the reverse journey, returning to his office. He told Valérie he'd be back later than usual, saying he had some work to finish up. She was disappointed that, on the day they had found each other again, he wasn't making an effort to get home early, but she assumed he didn't have any choice. In reality, he didn't do any work, didn't make any calls. His clients' problems were no longer his own. Floods, earthquakes, accidents of any kind … nothing could hurt him now.

His department was deserted. He left his office, went to the lift, and rode it up to Desjoyaux's floor. Once again he walked through the same long corridor he'd walked through a few hours before, but this time it didn't seem so long. Distances are always influenced by our state of mind. He spotted a cleaner in somebody's office and made sure she didn't see him. This wasn't difficult; she appeared to be performing her duties in a mechanical way, paying no attention to anything around her. Repetitive movements, the same every evening, struggling against exhaustion. She was the real Tom Cruise, thought Patrick, before continuing on his way. But before reaching Desjoyaux's office, he went to the back stairs and grabbed a fire extinguisher. Then he retraced his footsteps and headed towards the scene of his humiliation.

The door was open. He sat down for a moment in Desjoyaux's

chair, then swivelled around to look at the curtains. Those famous new curtains. A little earlier that afternoon, Patrick had bought a Zippo lighter at the bar. He flicked open the lid with his thumb – the gesture that can make any man look cool. Moreover, it was exactly the right tone for my hero's attitude. Some find grace in a mystical revelation; Patrick seemed to have undergone a nonchalance transplant. He was taking an insane risk (a security guard or another employee might pass by at any moment), but he appeared completely relaxed. In truth, he was acting like a man who has nothing left to lose.

He set fire to Desjoyaux's new curtains.

71

The curtains went up in flames. He watched them blaze, then used the fire extinguisher to put out the fire and calmly walked out of the office. Half an hour later, he was back at home. Valérie was reading in bed, waiting for him. He lay next to his wife and kissed her. The children were already in their rooms. Valérie asked him if he was hungry; he said he would take care of it. The two of them went to the kitchen and he made a cheese omelette. This ordinary evening felt like a new beginning.

As they told each other about their days, Patrick announced casually: 'He wanted to see me so I could give him my opinion on his curtains. Can you believe it? So I went back to his office this evening and I burned them.' She asked him to repeat this several times. Yes, she had heard correctly. She knew her husband, so she was well aware that he must have been at the very end of his tether to do something so reckless, so desperate, so brave. He told her in a whisper that it had been their discussion the previous night that had given him the strength to act; he didn't want to put up with it any more. Of course there would be consequences (Desjoyaux was bound to know it was him), but that no longer seemed important.

They suddenly started laughing hysterically. Deep down, she could understand him better than anyone. She wasn't being bullied, but it made her think of how colourless her life seemed. Daily existence had lost its flavour, so perhaps the solution was destruction? It was true that Valérie couldn't see herself smashing up the school library, but maybe she too needed to face up to the future in a less polite, less yielding way? A day before, she might well have been angry with her husband for jeopardising their way of life, for acting stupidly with no thought for the consequences, but everything was different now. She admired what he'd done, and it felt so good to admire her husband.

They went to their bedroom and made love. Patrick fell asleep, exhausted by the whirlwind of recent emotions. Valérie went back to the kitchen and called me. All of this was too crazy to keep to herself.

Never could I have imagined Patrick doing anything like that. It seemed obvious to me that my intrusion into this family had been a kind of trigger. Perhaps a writer should be parachuted into all dull situations? The more I thought about it, though, the more I saw things slightly differently. Yes, I was beginning to feel certain: any person you put in a book will start acting like a character in a novel.

WHAT I KNOW ABOUT MY CHARACTERS (4)

Madeleine Tricot. Nothing new. She must have been packing her suitcase. In two days we will leave for Los Angeles.

Patrick Martin. I could write a whole novel just on his day. Cried for the first time in years. Was reborn through his tears. I couldn't have imagined the story about the curtains. That Desjoyaux character is a real psychopath. Perfect for my book. Every good story needs a bad guy. And Patrick's reaction … crazy! I'm proud of him. He's bound to be dismissed for gross misconduct. He might even be prosecuted if the company presses charges.

Valérie Martin. What a turnaround! After announcing that she was going to divorce her husband, she's now fallen back in love with him. She must have been angry with Patrick for not being up to the task of daily existence. She probably never stopped loving him. I don't want to turn into a prophet of doom, but I do worry that her current euphoria might prove just as fleeting as her recent desire for divorce.

Jérémie Martin. Nothing new. I hope he at least got a good mark after my help.

Lola Martin. I don't know if our relationship can get any worse. She called me an idiot. Which I think is unfair. I simply tried to do what she asked me to do. Clément was annoyed by our meeting. Understandable: he doesn't see why his desire to have sex with Lola should be subject to my approval. Consequence: he dumped her. Maybe this is a tragedy or maybe it's a stroke of luck — who knows?

74

The next day was very strange. It was as if my characters were all having a day off from me. I waited to hear from them, but never did. In the end, I sent a message to Valérie, who sent me a terse: I'LL TELL YOU ALL ABOUT IT LATER. I have to admit one thing: there's a time for action, and a time for narration. I had to let the Martins live before transforming them into chapters.

At a loss (since the rest of my life was on pause), I went to visit Madeleine. She was fully focused on organising our expedition.[18] She didn't want to forget anything. She looked up at me then and said: 'This is probably the last suitcase I'll ever pack.' I can't think of many sentences that could move me like that one did. So there comes an age when every action, however banal, is accompanied by that thought: *this could be the last time*.

I told her to pack as much as she liked: I would be there to carry her luggage. To be honest, she didn't seem to be making much progress. She kept taking clothes from her wardrobe, then putting them back five minutes later. Madeleine was clearly anxious about what would happen in Los Angeles. The imminent reality had overturned her initial excitement. Now all she felt was apprehension. She was being buried under an avalanche of questions. Foremost among them: what does one wear to meet the love of one's life for the first time in sixty years? Surely he would be shocked by how old and wrinkled she was. It didn't even cross her mind that he was suffering the same anxieties.

18. For some people, packing a suitcase takes longer than the trip itself.

Yet again, in this endless echoing of love stories, I could understand her fears. How would I dress for my reunion with Marie? Simple and casual, to look relaxed. But maybe that would be understating the importance of the occasion. So ... a little smarter? Shirt and jacket? But that risked looking a bit pretentious. It's never a good sign once you start dithering. I should just follow my instincts. Besides, was this meeting ever actually going to happen? She still hadn't texted me, after all. Perhaps our nocturnal conversation had been merely a mirage.

That evening, I had nothing new to write about my characters. Valérie hadn't called me as she'd promised. Something must have happened after the episode of the burned curtains … but what? I felt like I'd come to the end of Season 1 of a new series, and I was going to have to wait weeks to find out what happened next. This is the great paradox of our era: since we have become used to getting everything we want immediately (there is no longer any delay between the desire and the fulfilment of that desire), the great modern enterprise consists in creating frustration. In fact, that is precisely what excites the consumer most: experiencing withdrawal symptoms. I was in exactly the same state. Desperate for my next fix of the Martins.

The next day, I went to pick up Madeleine and we got a taxi together to the airport. Just before boarding, I sent Valérie a message to let her know that all was well, but she didn't reply. She didn't even write to her mother to wish her a good flight. I was starting to find her silence a little worrying.

Once we were above the clouds, we ordered a glass of champagne each. Madeleine wanted this trip to be unforgettable. How could it be otherwise? Everything we were going through was an antidote to amnesia. The bubbles quickly went to my head, and my intoxication came as a relief. I love travelling, but I do tend to get quite stressed while I'm flying. I prefer the train. My ideal mode of transport would be railway tracks in the sky.

The flight attendant came up to me then and asked: 'Are you working on a new book?' I hesitated before answering. I always find it strange when people recognise me. It's true that some of my books have been successful, but it still strikes me as improbable. I wanted to say: 'Yes, it's sitting next to me,' but I didn't want to reveal anything about my current project. Generally, talking about a book when you're still working on it strikes me as a good way of killing it at birth. For every novel I've written, I've spent months without mentioning it to anyone. In the end, I told the flight attendant that I was taking a rest from fiction, and she told me I was right to *enjoy life*.

She went off to spread her good cheer among the other passengers before I had time to reply that I enjoyed life a lot more when I was working on a new book. Madeleine interrupted these existential reflections by asking me what meal I was going to choose. I hadn't even opened the menu yet.[19] After looking

19. Not that it mattered: the meat and the fish always taste exactly the same on aeroplanes.

through it, I went for the vegetarian option. Madeleine looked very happy as she told me that she'd chosen the same thing, as if this meant that we had the same view of life.

78

Prior to that moment, Madeleine had told me briefly about the trauma of Yves's departure, and the torments of her love for him, but I didn't know many details. I needed to gather more material before the reunion. And so, above the Atlantic, we travelled back into the past.

It had all started in a jazz club, although she couldn't remember its name. I mentioned a few legendary places such as Le Caveau de la Huchette or Le Duc des Lombards, but none of those names rang a bell for her. All she could tell me was that Miles Davis had played there, accompanied by Juliette Gréco, about ten years earlier. This wasn't particularly helpful: that famous couple had played most of Paris's big jazz clubs.

On the other hand, she could never forget that moment. As she was listening to the concert, she turned her head without really knowing why. Is it possible to sense the vibrations of a person who will stir our feelings before we even see them? As if the human body has a sort of emotional ESP. She noticed a shadowy male figure in a corner of the smoky cellar. All she could see of this man was his silhouette. He was smoking while calmly nodding his head. Madeleine felt helplessly drawn to that mysterious human form. She went over to him, pushing her way through the crowd of spectators. The frantic bebop rhythms gave the scene the feel of a fever dream. The closer she got to this man, the more clearly she could make out his face. Yves couldn't help but notice this young woman who was quite openly staring at him. Finally, they smiled at each other. Madeleine found an excuse for having walked over there: 'It's so hot in here. I needed to get some air.' And yet, if there was one place in the world where she found it hard to breathe, it was standing in front of this man. Exactly as if she'd spent her whole life running and then suddenly stopped.

Their first moment together began with a misunderstanding. Yves suggested they go outside to get some air. She thought he wanted to get her alone, when in fact he was just worried about this young woman who said she was suffocating. She remembered conversation being easy between them, as if they instinctively understood each other. In the end, they decided not to go back to the club, and went for a drink in a nearby bar instead. Caught up in the moment, Madeleine forgot to tell the girlfriend she'd gone to the club with about this change of plan. As for Yves, he'd gone there on his own to listen to the music, and that image suited him perfectly, thought Madeleine.

They quickly became inseparable. Yves was captivated by Madeleine's vivaciousness, her ability to make life more intense. He didn't realise that he was responsible for this; since meeting him, Madeleine felt she'd become *the best version of herself*. He loved their afternoons in bed, their bodies pressed together. Running his hands through her hair, he finally felt at home; his earthly wanderings had come to an end at the nape of her neck.

Normally a secretive man, Yves found himself opening up to Madeleine. He felt less reserved. His anxieties, and his blue moods, grew rarer as he discovered the simple joys of life. What more could anyone want from existence than the pleasure of a hot chocolate at the Café de Flore? Even then, it would sometimes cross his mind that this idyllic time would have to end at some point.

Madeleine was already working in the fashion industry, and

her heart would race when Yves came to fetch her from the atelier in the evenings. She now lived in constant anticipation of her moments with him. They would go to the cinema or for a walk, and the time would just fly by. Yves had received an inheritance after his father's death, and he wanted to write. He had tried poetry, novels, plays, even songs, before settling on screenplays. He was trying to create a film noir, and that was part of the reason he went to jazz clubs: in the hope of finding, if not inspiration, then at least an atmosphere. He would always slip to the back of the club to get a wide-angle view of the scene. Sometimes he would feel dejected, doubting his own talent. When he was in one of those moods, he preferred to be alone for days at a time. It drove Madeleine crazy to find herself in competition with her lover's writer's block. She tried to help him any way she could, racking her brains to come up with a nice line of dialogue or the start of an exciting action scene.

On several occasions during their affair, Madeleine had a strange feeling. She thought Yves was using his creative struggles as an alibi to avoid her.

Yves was sweet and attentive, but he never wanted to go on holiday, hated the idea of family meals, and believed that if they moved in together, it would mark the end of their honeymoon period. Madly in love, Madeleine accepted his artistic temperament, his odd wishes, as long as she felt her love was returned. And it was; there could be no doubt about that. Yves loved Madeleine, to the point that he was surprised, knocked off balance, even vexed by the strength of his feelings.

Two years went by that way, and maybe the third year too. Madeleine began to hope, with increasing intensity, that they would settle down together. She didn't dare admit to him that she would sometimes find herself thinking of names for their future children. Yves had always dodged such serious conversations, but one day he announced that he wasn't against the idea of marriage. It wasn't the most romantic declaration, admittedly, but – knowing her boyfriend well – Madeleine felt exultant. As he held her in his arms, he almost managed to imagine a different future. He always talked about his need for solitude, but was he sure he really had the right kind of mind to be an artist? His screenplay ideas never seemed to go anywhere, and his collaborations with others had produced nothing of note. Perhaps, for him, success was to be found in marital bliss. Of course, there was another factor that shouldn't be forgotten: he wanted to make Madeleine happy. His heart pounded at the sound of hers.

But things became complicated. As their wedding day grew closer, Yves began to think more and more often: 'I can't, I can't.' Finally he spoke those words aloud to Madeleine. She tried to reason with him, to persuade him, to understand him. In vain. His attitude made no sense to her. It was obvious that Yves wasn't a womaniser; he wasn't playing with her feelings. It hurt him to hurt her. And it hurt her to hurt him too. They were caught in a vicious circle of romantic suffering.

Without any real explanation, other than a vague feeling of unease and a desperate need to flee, he decided to leave for the United States. Without her. As she recounted the story's terrible denouement, the zenith of her despair, Madeleine started to hiccup. Decades later, the story of her devastation still had the unaltered taste of tragedy. I imagined that poor young woman living in a daze, suddenly severed from her *raison d'être*. Like a madwoman, she would return every night to the jazz club where they had met; and now I understood why she couldn't remember the name of the place – it had nothing to do with age or Alzheimer's. Amnesia has the benefit of making us forget any happiness that later turns to misery.

She didn't actually say this, but reading between the lines I gathered she'd attempted suicide at this point. Apparently, nobody knew about this; she'd never been able to talk about it. As a stranger, detached and objective, I was the first to hear Madeleine's dark secret. She survived, of course, but I think a part of her died during that period. The years passed, but the pain remained. The pain and the incomprehension. Not knowing something can drive you mad. She began to think the man she'd loved was a shadow (just as he had first appeared to her), the kind of creature that slips away if you get too close to it. Once she started thinking more clearly, she understood that he had not been fleeing her, but himself. Going to live on the other side of the world is never a casual decision. It is a way of abandoning the geographical part of who we are. Yves probably had no choice but to leave everything behind; no choice but to burn all his bridges. To put an end to the uncertainty that was causing them both immense pain. But he never explained why he'd gone. Our trip would finally allow Madeleine to write the last chapter in this unfinished novel.

A few years later, she had met René. Instead of passion, this was a choice based on reason. We won't go over that again. Suffice to say that René was a sort of human bandage. And Madeleine wanted children. She told me: 'I had the flu when René asked me to marry him. I was exhausted, bedridden. I wanted to throw up all the time, and that was when he got down on one knee and proposed.[20] I thought it was the most romantic thing he'd ever done.' I shared Madeleine's opinion on this. It is always charming to swim against the tide. René kept surprising me, and I was happy every time he reappeared in my book.

---

20. This was exactly what Alfred Hitchcock did. Perhaps René was inspired by the famous film director. On a ship, during a stormy Atlantic crossing, Alma – his future wife – was groaning in bed with seasickness. Hitchcock took advantage of this situation to ask: 'Will you marry me?' Later, he admitted to her: 'I thought I'd catch you when you were too weak to say no.'

At that precise moment, the flight attendant came over to ask us if we needed anything. Before leaving, she added: 'I love your stories about two Polish characters. It really makes me laugh, the fun you have with them!' Intrigued, Madeleine wanted to know more; the flight attendant's words had reminded her that I was not one of her friends, but a famous writer working on a new book. She admitted that she'd never read any of my work, and now she felt bad that she hadn't tried to find out more about me. But it suited me perfectly: I believed it was preferable that she knew nothing about me. She asked me about the two Poles, and I told her how the story began.

This was what had happened: for years, I had written out of passion or necessity, without thinking that one day I would manage to get published. The rejections piled up, and that seemed logical to me. I had no idea where my inspiration was leading me. That wasn't the point; for me, writing was the central activity of a parallel life. But the appearance of the two Poles changed everything. I wrote their story, and six months later I had a contract with a prestigious publishing firm. What had happened? I had the feeling that the two Poles had brought me luck, that they were responsible for the change in my fortunes. So I decided I would never write another book that did not feature, at some point, two Polish characters.

'So when will they appear in your book about me?' Madeleine asked. I frowned, perplexed. I hadn't thought about that. Since what I was writing wasn't fiction, I'd assumed I would have to sacrifice my Poles this time. But she was right: they had to be there, as always. I wanted to introduce them then and there, but how could I find two Polish people while flying over the Atlantic? I could hardly ask the flight attendant to make an announcement, the way you might if a passenger suddenly fell ill and you wanted to know if there was a doctor aboard the plane. 'Do we have two Polish people on the flight? If so, please contact your nearest flight attendant.'

In the end, I said to Madeleine: 'Would you mind if I wrote that there were two Polish people sitting next to us? Nobody would bother checking that.'

'No, that's fine.'

'Thank you.'

So we flew to Los Angeles beside two Polish people. At one point during the flight, I can't remember why, we exchanged a few words. They were both film directors. They'd studied at the famous film school in Łódź. They were going to Hollywood, where they hoped to sell a screenplay. One of them told me in English: 'It's an amazing story. Really amazing. We're sure it will make a remarkable film.' I was intrigued, of course, but they wouldn't tell me more than that. I hope with all my heart that, as I write these mythomaniacal lines now, they have managed to get their script into the hands of some important people, and that a big-name director wants to option it.

81

Two hours before we were due to land, Madeleine fell asleep. She slept so deeply that even heavy turbulence didn't wake her. I was afraid she would still be groggy when the flight attendant woke her up, but she was instantly back to normal and she admired the view through the window. While New York was a standing city, Los Angeles was more laid-back.[21] There was something magical about the sight of it.

We got through customs fairly quickly. The Americans are expert at managing the flow of tourists; you can see the same operation at work in queues at amusement parks. We ended up feeling disappointed when we got our passports stamped, because we'd almost come to believe that we were queuing up for a big wheel or a haunted house. Nowhere else on earth is the line between reality and entertainment so blurred. In certain American settings, it's impossible to know if what you're seeing is normal life or if someone is about to yell 'Action!'

We took a taxi to our hotel in Santa Monica. I'd chosen that location for its proximity to the ocean, of course, but also because it was close to where we would be meeting Yves the next morning. Our hotel was beautiful, if a little faded. I wish I could put a Doors song in the background to this paragraph, but unfortunately literature is silent.

We went to our rooms, and Madeleine decided to go to bed straight away. It was only six in the evening, so I wanted to stay

21. It looked like a city sprawled out on a lounger.

awake as long as I could to avoid feeling jet-lagged the next morning. I went for a walk; the air was so warm. I couldn't believe we were already here. I stood facing an enormous red sun as it disappeared into the Pacific, but I still had the taste of Paris in my mouth.

82

A little later, I lay on my bed. There's a huge pleasure in feeling crushed by fatigue. Insomniacs must feel as if they are jet-lagged all the time. Just as my eyelids started to droop, my phone rang. I'd left a message with Valérie to tell her we'd arrived safely, but I hadn't expected her to call me back so early (it was 6 a.m. in France).

She wanted to know everything about the journey: the hotel, the atmosphere, my conversations with her mother ... It was very bad timing, from my point of view. There's a kind of torture in being forced to stay awake just as you are falling asleep. But I did feel relieved that she'd finally called me. And, most pressingly, I wanted to know what had happened with Patrick. I'd been thinking about that storyline constantly for the past two days. How had Desjoyaux reacted when he found his curtains burned? Valérie told me he'd been stunned. Several witnesses confirmed that he hadn't spoken at all for quite a long time afterwards. It wasn't merely an act of vandalism; he saw it as a violent personal attack, almost a death knell.

Desjoyaux knew perfectly well what he was doing to his employees, but he could never have imagined that his behaviour would provoke such an act. Before that, nobody had ever fought back or even reacted at all to his sadism. The fear of losing their job had always kept his victims silent and docile. This time, it was different. He had caught Patrick at the worst moment of his life. At a moment when he had no choice but to react. Filled with a new energy, refusing to accept defeat, Patrick had overcome his fear of the consequences. Because he knew there would be consequences. Desjoyaux couldn't doubt for a minute the identity of the arsonist; it was Martin, it had to be Martin.

At last he got a grip on himself and summoned the employee who had dared to defy him. Several minutes passed, but Patrick did not appear. Desjoyaux yelled at his secretary to call Patrick again (it was completely out of character for him to lose his temper).

On the other end of the line, she heard a man say: 'If he wants to talk to me, tell him to come here ...' Odile, the secretary, asked Patrick to repeat what he'd said. And he did: 'If he wants to talk to me, tell him to come here ...'

Odile told him she couldn't report this kamikaze response to her boss. Particularly since Desjoyaux was standing there watching her, waiting for her to confirm his attacker's imminent arrival. But Martin hung up, so Odile had no choice but to repeat what she'd heard. She opened her mouth but no sound emerged: some sentences are so afraid of the reactions they will provoke that they prefer to announce themselves in silence. Odile had to try several times before her voice grew loud enough to be heard:

'He said that if you want to talk to him, you have to go and see him ...'

She lowered her head then, as if her boss were pointing a revolver at her.

In the end, Desjoyaux went to look for Martin's office. But, since he didn't know where it was and he didn't want to have to speak to anyone, he walked more than half a mile through the building's corridors. Everyone turned to stare at him as he passed, and he seemed to hear the word 'curtains' whispered everywhere he went. Or was that his imagination? When you feel guilty, your mind supplies voices of denunciation. He was a

219

Raskolnikov of curtains. At last he found Martin's office. Patrick said hello first – the cherry on the cake of his rebellion. Shocked and sweating, Desjoyaux shouted: 'Do you realise what you've done?'

'What are you talking about?'

'You know very well what I'm talking about. It has to be you. The curtains!'

'Why does it have to be me?'

'Because we talked about them that afternoon, and ... Oh, I don't have to justify myself to you! I just came to tell you that I am firing you for gross misconduct.'

'What about my clients?'

'I don't give a damn about your clients. We'll just give them to someone else. They won't even notice the difference. There's another Martin in accounts – I'll give him your job. That way, the clients will never know anything's changed!'

'And when do I have to leave?'

'Now, you idiot! Now!'

'You really think it's normal to ask a senior executive who's been at the company for twenty years what he thinks of your curtains? When you've told him three days before that it's *imperative* you see him? You think that's normal?'

'I don't care! What's not normal is setting fire to my curtains! So get out of here now!'

'All right. But this is just the beginning.'

'What does that mean? Are you threatening me, Martin? Are you threatening me?'

'It doesn't mean anything. You can take it any way you want.'

'You madman! I'll be back in an hour and I don't want to see the slightest trace of your presence here. And believe me, you can forget about getting a single centime in compensation. I hope I see you one day begging in the street.'

'That's not in my plans. But thank you for your concern about my future.'

Desjoyaux stood there for a moment, staggered by this man's recklessness, then he left.

All Patrick's colleagues watched him admiringly. They couldn't believe it. Was this the same man? He felt happy that he'd done what he'd decided, without wavering. But what good would it do him now? He would be getting home at ten in the morning on a weekday, with two boxes filled with souvenirs of his career. Only two boxes after so many years. As he cleared his desk, people came by to congratulate him on his bravery. But would they still be thinking about him ten days from now? Or even two days from now? Probably not. His act of rebellion had thrilled them all, but it wouldn't have any lasting effect. His heroism was a dead end too. What would become of him now? Everyone knew everyone else in the insurance business. Word of his gross misconduct would spread quickly. People always leap to conclusions. Whatever his reasons, it looked like an act of insanity. They would think: if he was being bullied, he should have filed a complaint. Only a madman would get revenge like that. Yes, it seemed obvious to him now: by burning those curtains, he had torched his own career. His wife would be proud of him, of course. He could sail on the calm seas of her admiration for a while, but sooner or later he would crash into the rocks of reality. And the gloomy future that awaited him. His euphoria was evaporating around him and he was starting to bitterly regret his rash act. He would pay a heavy price for those few moments of insurrection.[22]

---

22. For readers who like Patrick, and who applauded his crazy bravery, let me reassure you now: things will not turn out the way he imagines.

83

The advantage of that long phone call with Valérie was that it enabled me to go to bed a bit later. Not that it prevented me being wide awake in the middle of the night. I passed the time by watching television. Mostly game shows, with the contestants yelling all the time. In the United States, all participants on such programmes require a PhD in hysteria. When I went downstairs, about six in the morning, I found Madeleine already sitting in the breakfast room. She, too, had woken very early. Our meeting was at nine, and the wait seemed endless. I could feel her tension. She must have been wondering if she'd done the right thing by coming here. Strangely, she admitted to me that she was thinking about her husband. She almost felt as if she were being unfaithful to him. Everything was mixed up in her head.

I suggested we go for a walk on the beach to unwind. The sunrise was witnessed by an army of joggers. How is it humanly possible to do physical exercise that early in the morning? If you go out in Paris at that time of day, you're more likely to find drunk people coming out of nightclubs. The dawn joggers, mingled with my jet lag, made the moment seem slightly surreal.

Suddenly, Madeleine said: 'Are you sure he'll be there?'

'Yes, I told him we'd arrived last night. He's expecting us.'

'What if it's not him? Just someone who resembles him.'

'That seems unlikely …'

'What if we have nothing to say to each other?'

'Then you'll just look at each other in silence, I suppose.'

'What if we can't see each other because we have blurred vision?'

'...'

I thought that last question was a joke, but apparently I was wrong. She was too on edge to be capable of humour. She was genuinely afraid she might lose it completely; just sit there tongue-tied or half blind. I could sense her growing ever more rigid. I even thought I could hear the dryness in her mouth. She reminded me of an actor with stage fright. This was the film of her life that was about to play before my eyes; the fiction that all love is.

It was so intense that I began to have doubts myself. Suddenly, I feared my presence would be intrusive. I wanted to write about reality, not steal their privacy. Some things are too beautiful to be seen by outsiders. Madeleine could tell me all about it afterwards, if she wanted to. Yes, that would be better. I would accompany her to the meeting, then leave her there. Would it really matter if my book didn't contain a first-hand description of the scene? Everyone could imagine it. Each reader could create his or her own reunion novel. Just as I was ready to tell Madeleine about my decision, she took my hand and said: 'I want you to stay. I need you.'

We arrived an hour early at the meeting place: a large café divided into two rooms by a glass wall. Yves was already there. A shame: I'd wanted to write the scene of his arrival. My first impression was that he looked incredibly elegant. Dressed in a linen suit, wearing a large hat, he was like a character from a Fitzgerald novel. He quickly thanked me for organising this reunion, before focusing his full attention on Madeleine. So I took a few steps back to let them experience this moment that I, for one, would never be able to forget.

For a few days now, I had felt a very close connection with Madeleine. We were united by my project, and I had a front-row seat in the theatre of her emotions. This woman and this man looked at each other, hardly even believing what they were seeing. Their eyes were wet with tears, but their smiles were wide. For a few seconds, they were unable to touch each other. That's what moved me most, I think. Seeing them like that, face to face, frozen in amazement.

Finally they hugged and exchanged a few polite greetings. Yves was worried that the trip had been too tiring, and Madeleine reassured him. She would probably be exhausted later, but for now she was high on adrenaline. They turned to me then, like children looking for instructions from an adult. This was their story. I told them I was going to sit outside. I even wondered if Yves had chosen this place especially for me. I could sit on the veranda, on the other side of the glass divider, and observe them without disturbing them.

As implausible as this may seem, Marie sent me a message just as I was taking my seat. It was as if she were looking down on me kindly from above. She appeared on my phone screen as I watched an image of eternal love. Should I see this as a sign? How could I not? It was like an emotional echo.

Marie asked simply how I was. I told her what I was witnessing just then. THAT'S AN INCREDIBLE STORY, she replied. I WOULD HAVE LOVED TO TAKE A PHOTOGRAPH OF THEIR REUNION ... I didn't mention this before, but Marie is a photographer. In fact, we first met at one of her exhibitions. I didn't want to talk about myself in this book, but do I really have a choice now?

I'd had no desire to go to that private view. But that's always how people meet each other: when they don't feel like going out. I'd gone with a film director who I was hoping would adapt one of my novels. When he suggested that I accompany him to that gallery, I thought it would be an opportunity to get to know him better, helping our future collaboration. But nothing went the way I'd anticipated. As soon as we arrived, he disappeared into a crowd of other acquaintances and I was left on my own. The gallery was composed of a number of small rooms, so it felt like drifting from one cocoon to another. I decided I should take a brief look at the photographs, out of politeness, and then go home. I didn't know who the photographer was, and I didn't really care. I'd never thought much of photography as an art anyway (Marie would change my mind on this, of course), and

I wandered from picture to picture in a rather nonchalant way.

Gradually, however, something strange happened. With each successive image, I felt increasingly captivated by the artist's work. After a while, I found myself standing motionless in front of a photograph. It was a frame with the word '*Oui*' written inside it. I couldn't have explained why, but I was deeply moved. Maybe I was affected by the pure expression of simplicity. I stood there for a moment, reading and rereading that yes, until I heard a voice behind me say: 'It's a pleasant surprise to see you here.' I turned around then and saw Marie. Before I could reply, she went on to say that she'd loved one of my novels. My first impression of her was of a human version of that 'yes'. She struck me as happy and radiant; a far cry from the standard image of the anxious artist at the opening of their exhibition. I said something like this to her, and she responded: 'Oh, I have nothing to worry about tonight! Everyone is going to tell me that my work is wonderful! Even you … I imagine you really liked it?' It was difficult to tell how much irony there was behind these words, but I adored the way she didn't take herself too seriously. So I answered her question by pointing to her photograph.

Oui.

Yes, I really liked her work. And yes, I wanted to see this woman again. That was obvious. I am not usually very forward with women, but I asked her if she was free one night to go out for a drink with me. She looked at me without speaking, then she in turn raised her finger to the yes on the wall.

86

During my previous text conversation with Marie, we'd just talked about the idea of seeing each other again. We hadn't really talked about our lives. This time, she wrote that her new exhibition was opening in two days and she hoped I would come. Two days, I repeated mentally. I'd arrived in Los Angeles the day before, and that would mean having to leave the next day. It seemed absurd to travel all that way for such a short stay. And I couldn't leave Madeleine here all alone. Not to mention the fact that I was writing a book about her. These thoughts collided in my head, briefly confusing me. Within a few seconds, though, I was replying that her timing was perfect because I was returning to France the next day and I'd be happy to be there to support her on her big day.

I'd made my decision, and my heart sped at the thought of it while I continued to observe Yves and Madeleine. They were deep in conversation. Madeleine seemed troubled by what she was hearing, and their faces looked a little tense to me; I had no idea what he might be telling her. Two or three times, she turned towards me, to check that I was still there. I gave a friendly wave in response. Since their discussion showed no signs of ending, I started to read *USA Today*. I wished I'd brought my laptop with me so I could do some writing while I waited for them.

*

We tend to remember each person's final image. When we think of Lagerfeld, we immediately see that tall, slender man. A figure destined to become a logo. We forget that for several years the designer was overweight. It is strange seeing pictures from that era. Given the way he comes across – that aura of absolute self-control – it is hard to imagine that this man ever struggled with his weight. But he did. He even came up with a wonderful weight-loss aphorism: 'Dieting is the only game you win by losing.' So he saw it as a game, but who were the players? From what Madeleine revealed to me of his personality, I have the impression it was more a show that he performed for the benefit of his court of commentators. So, he spectacularly lost six and a half stone in the space of a few months. With him, everything was the stuff of legend. He couldn't allow himself the slightest mediocrity. He worked on his diet with the same intensity he brought to his designs. He wanted everyone to talk about it. I even wondered if perhaps he'd deliberately put on weight purely so he could enjoy watching everyone's amazement at his subsequent weight loss. He wrote a book about it afterwards. As a marketing genius, he made his body a bankable image. Didn't his silhouette end up on cans of Coca-Cola? That is what I find most fascinating about Lagerfeld: he himself was his greatest creation.

At last, they beckoned me inside. Yves immediately caught hold of me. 'So you're Madeleine's biographer!'

'Yes, I'm writing about her.'

'There must be so much to say, I imagine. Well, if you need me, I can tell you a few good stories.'

'No, you can keep that to yourself,' said Madeleine without managing to smile; she seemed to have been affected by the tenor of their conversation.

'I suggested that we all have lunch at my place,' Yves went on. 'But Madeleine wants to get some rest. Which is perfectly understandable. So you can drop by later. My apartment isn't far from here. It's not a big place, but it has a nice view.'

'Yes, let's do that. We'll go back to the hotel, and I'll call you later,' I said, sounding like a tour guide.

They embraced tightly, as if afraid they wouldn't see each other for another sixty years. I said we could take a taxi, but Madeleine wanted to walk. I was eager to question her, of course, but I sensed this wasn't the right time. Though usually so chatty, she was silent now. Just before leaving her outside her room, I had to tell her that I was going to change the date of my flight – and that I'd be flying back to France the next day. She immediately asked me if something was wrong. I told her, without any dramatic intonation, that I had something that needed attending to urgently. She respected my wish not to say anything more than that, and did not seem at all worried by the idea of remaining here alone for a few days. It was clear that Yves would take care of her. Things would be better like that, I thought, without their literary chaperone.

87

I took a nap in my room then, and when I woke up it was mid-afternoon: already very late in France. I called Valérie to update her on what was happening. For the first time, she was angry. I reassured her by telling her it was for the best, and that Yves was absolutely charming. But she believed I was being irresponsible: taking her mother to the other side of the world, then abandoning her there alone. Not only that, but she was a sick woman. I told her I had never seen Madeleine looking weak or unwell. On the contrary, in fact, she had always struck me as very lively and dynamic. But Valérie continued hurling abuse at me: 'You're leaving my mother alone there!' I thought I heard Patrick's voice then. Valérie asked him to repeat what he'd just said, and I heard him say: 'Why don't we fly out?' The school holidays started the next day, and he was unemployed. It had been so long since the two of them had gone away together. And by going there to accompany Madeleine, they would have time to rediscover each other a little more. Valérie grew calm as she thought about this possibility; perhaps the announcement of my early departure was a sign, after all. They could try to find a flight on Saturday; they had some savings; now was the time to use them. And their children were old enough to be left on their own; in fact, they'd be thrilled to have the apartment to themselves.

Valérie sent me a message ten minutes later, informing me that they'd bought tickets for Sunday. I could tell Madeleine, who would probably be surprised by this turn of events. But then there had already been so many improbable episodes in the past few days. Valérie would no doubt find it moving to meet her mother's first love. Perhaps, like me, she would see it as *The Bridges of Madison County* with a happy ending. A love affair, a separation, years of frustration, but with this reunion as its climax. On the veranda, behind the glass divider that looked a bit like a cinema screen, I'd thought to myself that Meryl Streep had just found Clint Eastwood.

I suggested that I visit them on Saturday after arriving in Paris so I could tell them all about the trip. This was my alibi for meeting up with the whole Martin family, probably for the last time. I asked Valérie to make sure the children were there, though I doubted Lola would agree to see me. I had sent her a photograph of her grandmother standing in front of the Pacific (a symbolic name for this pictorial peace offering), but she hadn't replied. Apparently I had a better rapport with old people. This chimed with a feeling I'd always had about myself: that I was born old. In fact, it was more than a feeling, because my life had provided proof of it: as a teenager, I'd suffered a cardiac disease that generally only affects the elderly. The doctors had observed me and analysed me, like a rare medical specimen. So, clearly, old age flows through my veins. But that is a different book.

88

Late that afternoon, Madeleine called my room. She was waiting for me in the lobby. I went downstairs and, before even mentioning her conversation with Yves, told her that her daughter would be arriving on Sunday. She replied instantly: 'I would have been fine staying here on my own.' Clearly it annoyed her that her family had organised a sort of rescue party; I think she felt she was being treated like an invalid.

'Patrick and Valérie are going to turn it into a holiday,' I explained.

'Oh really? He's coming too?' she asked, surprised. It had been a long time since she'd seen the two of them together, apart from the odd birthday party. I omitted to mention the cremation of the curtains or Patrick's dismissal. Madeleine had been through enough exciting adventures recently.

We left the hotel and went for a walk, in search of a bench facing the ocean.

'I told Yves I'd see him tomorrow morning instead of later today,' she told me.

'That's fine.'

'With the jet lag, I'm finding it hard to think clearly. I probably need to digest everything we discussed this morning.'

'Do you want to talk about it?'

'Yes, I'm going to tell you.'

And yet she fell silent after pronouncing those words, waiting for us to find the perfect spot for the sharing of secrets.

A few minutes later, we were sitting side by side. She began by telling me what she'd found out. Her first words were: 'He's homosexual.' I said nothing for a moment; that possibility had crossed my mind. It seemed obvious now. Madeleine repeated several times that she had been blind. Maybe it was the times. The fact that she was fairly innocent about life. And Yves had never talked about it. Their sex life had seemed more than satisfying to her, but she had nothing to compare it to, no way of understanding a man's feelings. So that was the reason for his discontent. He was happy with Madeleine, but he knew he was living a lie.

Yves had told her everything; he'd been totally frank, even at the risk of offending her. He even admitted that during their relationship he'd had affairs with men. Often they were married men, fathers. Yves had imagined that, like them, he'd be able to lead a sort of double life. Particularly since he had very deep feelings for Madeleine. He thought he could have a classic married life, and a gay sex life in parallel. That was why he'd agreed to marry her. But something had held him back from following this path. He couldn't base his existence on a lie, couldn't betray the woman he loved. Several times, he'd tried to tell her about it, but the words had refused to emerge from his mouth. Towards the end of their affair, he'd fallen ill. Madeleine had forgotten that episode, having shrouded the entire period in a kind of mental fog. But Yves had been bedridden for several weeks with a fever, his body poisoned by the truth he couldn't reveal.

He had to get away. Of course, he knew that Madeleine would be devastated, just as he himself was. And he knew how awful it was to leave her without any explanation for his departure. But the confession would not come out. He was afraid that, if he told her everything, she would regard their love as a farce. By keeping silent, he believed he could preserve the beauty of what they'd shared. But, in fact, he'd done something much worse by abandoning her in silence. He had made her so miserable that she'd wanted to kill herself. He realised that now, but he begged her to understand that it had been impossible for him to act in any other way. So they had embraced, before signalling to me that it was time to join them.

I was deeply moved by the calm way Madeleine told me all this. She was relieved to finally be able to put into words the abandonment that had haunted her throughout her life. Yves had wanted to tell her the truth when he returned to Paris, years later, but she'd refused to see him. So she had missed the chance to hear his explanation. Madeleine needed time to digest what she'd heard, but it was clear that she and Yves were happy to be reunited; happy and stunned by this strange twist of fate.

I can say it now: Madeleine would end up spending a whole month in Los Angeles. And their separation didn't last long, because Yves would come to visit her in Paris the following summer. The three of us would have dinner together. They would continue to tell me stories from their past, but by then I had already finished writing my book. Perhaps Madeleine would slowly lose her memory, but to this point she still seems to me perfectly lucid and full of life. What if this adventure had woken in her brain the missing part of her memory? Or perhaps it was, once again, the power of literature? I don't know. All I know is that, during the dinner we had together, Yves told her that she was the love of his life.

For now, it was early morning, and I had just landed in Paris. I took a taxi to the Martins' apartment. I had no idea what was going to happen or who would be there to welcome me. I was surprised to discover all four of them sitting at the table, waiting to have breakfast with me.

Even more surprisingly, it was Jérémie who spoke first: 'Since you entered our lives, my parents have started loving each other again, my sister has become depressed, my grandmother's gone to Los Angeles, and I've become popular. What exactly were you trying to achieve?' This final question reminded me of something Lola had said, albeit more aggressively. It didn't seem to require a response; it was more of an observation, really. I didn't understand what he meant about being popular though. 'I still can't believe it …' he said, handing me his phone. There, I saw a video of him, already shared more than 100,000 times. And no, I did not imagine any of those zeroes.

'It's completely crazy,' Valérie agreed.

This was what had happened. The day he was fired, Patrick told his children everything. They had a sort of emergency family meeting. He detailed the humiliations and the psychological violence he'd suffered at the hands of his boss. Although it had been mentioned in passing during our first dinner together, this was the first time Jérémie and Lola had truly understood their father's increasingly withdrawn behaviour. It helped them all immensely to put a chaotic situation into words. Still high on his new energy, Patrick had no hesitation in sharing the story of burning the curtains. His children listened to this account in amazement. They both regarded it as an act of heroism, irrespective of the consequences. Patrick might have lost his job, but he had won his children's undying admiration.

An hour later, Jérémie had posted a video on his social networks, in which he expressed how proud he felt of his father for fighting back against his bully of a boss. He added two hashtags to his post: #JeSuisPatrickMartin and #BalanceTonPatron, the latter a reference to #BalanceTonPorc, the French version of #MeToo. The video was quickly shared by hundreds of other users, racking up an impressive number of views. Many other people shared their stories of workplace bullying; inspired by this new spirit of solidarity, they'd found the courage to tell all. Once the stories went public, the risk of reprisals was obviously reduced. It was a sort of small revolution for France's employees.

In less than two days, it had already become a phenomenon. Several journalists tried to contact the teenage boy who had started the movement, along with his father. And it wouldn't end there. The movement grew so big that the insurance company had no choice but to reinstate Patrick … and to fire Desjoyaux, of course. So the world of social media has an upside. There were consequences, however: the story's fame meant Patrick could never be free of it. For years, whenever he went to visit a client, they would always ask him with a little smile: 'And our curtains? What do you think?'

Although she had agreed to take part in the meeting, Lola refused to meet my eye. She didn't seem as hostile as before, however. Her anger was fading. She admitted that it wasn't my fault Clément had dumped her. Plus, her doubts had been justified. He'd immediately started seeing another girl. Lola had sent me on a mission to pin down the slipperiest teenage boy imaginable. Not only had the story not proved very exciting, but it saddened me that this was Lola's only connection with my book. She would remain my great regret. But maybe one day I would return to write another book about the Martins, and then she would be my priority. What would become of her? The future is an unwritten book.

It was time to bring things to an end. Of course I could have continued following the Martin family, but I don't like books over 300 pages long. That was sufficient reason to pause our relationship. We said our goodbyes quite warmly, and in the end they all thanked me. Out on the landing, I turned back. I wanted to immortalise this moment with a photograph. They kindly indulged my last wish. As the four of them sat on the living-room sofa, trying to smile naturally, I looked at my heroes.

THE MARTINS

EPILOGUE

1

I tried to take a nap that afternoon so I'd be rested for the evening, but I couldn't fall asleep. I was too excited. I was about to see Marie again, and in the ideal setting too. The private view for her new art exhibition brought us back full circle to our first meeting. And you know I like my books to be round.

2

I'd attempted to find out more information on her new exhibition, but there was nothing online. For years, we had shared everything; she followed the progress of my novels, and I watched enthusiastically as her projects developed. I liked the idea that we were living parallel creative lives, without occupying the same artistic terrain. She worked with images and I worked with words. There was something complementary about this, a synergy. I admired her capacity to reinvent herself, to constantly seek out new ideas. I really missed her vivaciousness.

The invitation to her private view was a very positive sign. She'd told me: 'It would be lovely if you could be there.' It was such an important event for her; despite the separation, there are moments when you can't live without each other.

I was relieved that our reunion would take place in that context. I think it would have been intimidating to meet her alone in a café, after so much time. It takes far more effort to be charming while seated than while standing. And what time of day would we have chosen? A lunch was too impersonal, in my opinion. A coffee in the afternoon? Even worse. Drinks in the early evening were fine, but less appealing than dinner. By inviting me to her private view, she had avoided the whole 'time of day' problem. We could skip straight to the pleasure of seeing each other again. But I was so anxious about what would happen. Never before had I felt as if I was about to go on a first date with a woman I was already in love with.

There were lots of people there when I arrived. I stood for a moment on the other side of the road, observing the gallery through the window. I kept expecting her to suddenly appear from the crowd of guests. And a few minutes later, that was exactly what happened; her face became visible between two shoulders. Everyone was talking to her, trying to monopolise her, but I hoped she was waiting for me. It was so intense, seeing her again, knowing she was so close, and in my mind's eye I saw Yves and Madeleine, behind that glass wall. Once again, I was a spectator. But this time, I had to enter the scene of the film. I had my own role to play.

Inside the gallery, I wandered between photographs. The tone of her pictures was even more joyful than usual. In fact, the exhibition's title was *Happiness*. She had tried to capture instants of joy wherever she could find them. One of the photographs showed a family of four all smiling on their living-room sofa, and I couldn't help thinking about the picture of the Martins I'd just taken. Yet another echo between art and life.

After a while, I finally managed to fight my way through the crowd to Marie. We embraced warmly, even though the idea of politely kissing her on the cheeks left me dejected. The conversation between us flowed immediately, and she told me again how happy she was that I'd made it to her private view. I was able to congratulate her, but soon after that she was swept away by other well-wishers. She just had time to ask: 'Are you staying for a while?' I nodded. I would stay for a while, and probably longer.

Yes, definitely longer. It felt so intense, seeing her again. I'd managed to appear relaxed, to hide my body's faint trembling, but I couldn't lie to myself any longer: I had been yearning for and dreaming of this moment for months. The novel of our reunion was the only exception to my fictional drought. I would sometimes have long, imaginary conversations with Marie. And now here she was, a few feet away from me. If she let me close to her again, what would we do? I hoped we could go away somewhere. The destination didn't matter. Everything would be different now. My experience with the Martins had given me a better understanding of the passing of time, the urgency of what really mattered. I'd realised that life remained the most powerful antidote to fiction. I wanted to hold Marie's hand, to feel its reality in mine.

5

An hour later, there weren't quite so many people in the gallery's various rooms. I was looking at a photograph when I heard Marie's voice behind me. Just like our first time. I loved this echo so much that I turned around slowly. But when I saw her, she was standing next to a man.

'You still like it?'

'Yes … yes …'

'I wanted to introduce you to Marc.'

'Hello …'

'Hello …'

We shook hands, and Marc said he had a call to make, then left us alone.

'Who's that?' I asked.

'I didn't want to tell you by text, but I met Marc a few months ago.'

'Are you happy?' I managed to ask.

'Yes. We've moved in together.'

'Already?'

'It all happened very quickly, and …'

'And what? You're pregnant?'

'Yes.'

'…'

'I didn't know how to tell you.'

'So now I understand why the exhibition's called *Happiness*.'

'Maybe.'

'Well, congratulations. I hope you'll be very happy,' I said, trying desperately to conceal my true feelings.

'Anyway, I'm really glad you came.'

'That's okay. I couldn't miss this. But I should be going now.'

'You don't want to stay for a drink?'

'No, I'm feeling a bit jet-lagged.'

'Oh yeah … your story of the grandmother. I can't wait to hear how that ends!'

We hugged goodbye, and I left the gallery.

Outside on the street, I read the title of the exhibition one last time:

HAPPINESS

6

I would have preferred a different ending for my book, but that's life. I felt stupid for having believed my own fantasies. I walked home through the night, and for an instant I thought about calling Valérie and telling her what had happened. But there wasn't much to say, really. I'd written a novel in my head. Marie and I had exchanged a few friendly text messages, and she'd told me it would make her happy if I could attend her private view. All perfectly pleasant. And that was all. But I had dreamed up a whole new chapter between us. Perhaps that meant I was capable of writing fiction again after all.